D0564159

THE WRECK OF THE *GOLDEN MARY*

John Dujan

The
WRECK
of the
GOLDEN MARY

By

Charles Dickens

and

Wilkie Collins

With Illustrations by John Dugan and an Introduction by
Herbert van Thal

LIBRARY PUBLISHERS
NEW YORK

Published in 1956 by Library Publishers, Inc.
8 West 40th Street, New York 18, N.Y.

Originally published in the Christmas
issue of *Household Words* (1856)

MADE AND PRINTED IN GREAT BRITAIN FOR
LIBRARY PUBLISHERS
BY MORRISON AND GIBB LIMITED, LONDON AND EDINBURGH

CONTENTS

PART ONE

PART TWO

PART THREE

INTRODUCTION

DICKENS was a man of overwhelming energy, and he enjoyed being in touch with as many facets of human activity as he could. Hence his appetite and love for Editorship. He had served ten years' apprenticeship on Forster's *The Examiner* and he worked on the *Morning Chronicle*. He had slaved away assimilating material for the *Daily News*, but he resigned the Editorship three weeks before the first number appeared.[1] He had before thinking of Household Words launched the unsuccessful Master Humphrey's Clock. But it was never for long that Dickens' mind was not simmering on something new. In September 1845 he wrote to Forster: "The old notion of the Periodical which has been agitating itself in my mind for so long, I really think is at last gradually growing into form . . . a weekly journal, price either three half-pence or two pence,

[1] No explanation of his own conduct on this occasion was ever offered by Dickens, and no satisfactory explanation of it had been offered by any of his biographers. It was obvious that he was competent to edit a paper: and if his abandonment of the *Daily News* is contrasted with the energy he displayed in relation to Household Words it seems likely that what Dickens really wanted was a vehicle for the expression of his own feeling about life. Symons: Dickens p. 21. 1951.

matter in part original, and in part selected, and always having if possible a little good poetry." To this idea Forster was doubtful and it was not until 1849 that *The Shadow*, as Dickens first wished to call his paper, became the substance and a preliminary announcement was made towards the end of 1849. Finding a name for the journal caused a lot of thought, *Household Voice*, *Guest and Face*, as well as *The Comrade, The Microscope, The Highway of Life, The Lever, The Rolling Years* and *The Holly Tree* (with two lines of Southey for a motto) were some of the suggested titles.[1] Finally the quotation from Henry IV, Act IV, Scene III was chosen, though as Fitzgerald tells us it was misquoted in the title page as "Familiar in their mouths as Household Words." Bradbury and Evans, to whom Dickens now gave everything he wrote, were to be the publishers, and Forster suggested an assistant, one William Henry Wills— something of a "character" a little pragmatical, taking his office *au grand serieux*, rather *au plus grand*, something of a cockney and with a persuasion that he had a fund of humour.[2] Dickens enjoyed working with Wills and was delighted in his odd and eccentric ways, though apparently Forster did not share this liking—which was mutual.[3]

The offices were in a rather pretty little building at No. 16 Wellington Street. One of the first persons

---

[1] Kitton. Minor Writings of Dickens. p. 110.
[2] Fitzgerald. Memories of Charles Dickens. p. 119.
[3] Idem. p. 119.

whose services Dickens enlisted was Mrs. Mary Howitt—
a writer no doubt completely forgotten to-day and yet
one of considerable interest, and although the inclusion
of her name in this brief introduction may seem a little
wide of the mark, few accounts of Dickens have given
much notice to her. Mary Howitt was born in 1799 of
a prosperous Quaker family in Uttoxeter in Stafford-
shire and her mother was a descendant of Andrew Wood,
the same who was attacked by Swift in the Drapier
letters. Along with her husband with whom she col-
laborated she made known to English readers the whole
of Frederika Bremer's Works, she translated Hans
Christian Andersen's autobiography, she wrote an
incessant number of children's books and with her
husband started Howitt's Journal of Literature and
Popular Progress (1847).

It was on February 20th, 1850, that Dickens wrote to
her: "You may have seen the first dim announcements
of the new cheap, literary weekly journal I am about to
start. Frankly, I want to say to you, that if you would ever
write for it you would delight me, and I should consider
myself very fortunate indeed in enlisting your assistance.

"I propose to print no names of contributors, either
in your own case or any other, and to give established
writers the power of reclaiming their papers after a
certain time. I hope any connection with the enterprise
would be satisfactory and agreeable to you in all respects,
as I should most earnestly endeavour to make it. If I
wrote a book, I could say no more than I mean to

9

suggest to you in these few lines. All that I leave unsaid, I leave to your generous understanding."[1]

Household Words was launched! and the first number appeared on the 30th March 1850, price 2d. "We aspire," wrote Dickens "to live in the Household affections, and to be numbered among the Household thoughts of our readers. We hope to be the comrade and friend of many thousands of people of both sexes,[2] and of all ages and conditions, on whose faces we may never look. We seek to bring into innumerable homes, from the shining world around us, the knowledge of many social wonders, good and evil, that are not calculated to render any of us less ardently persevering in ourselves, less tolerant of another, less faithful in the progress of mankind, less thankful for the privilege of living in the summer-dawn of time.

"No mere utilitarian spirit, no iron binding of the mind to grim realities, will give a harsh tone to our Household Words. In the bosoms of the young and old, of the well-to-do and of the poor, we would tenderly cherish that light of Fancy which is inherent in the human breast; which, according to its nurture, burns with an inspiring flame, or sinks into a sullen glare but which (or woe betide that day!) can never be extinguished. To show to all, that in all familiar things, even in those which are repellent on the surface, there is Romance enough, if we will find it out; to teach the

[1] Fitzgerald, *Memories of Charles Dickens*, p. 128.
[2] This proved to be so.

hardest workers at this whirling wheel of toil, that their lot is not necessarily a moody, brutal fact, excluded from the sympathies and graces of imagination, to bring the greater and the lesser in degree, together, upon that wide field, and mutually dispose them to a better acquaintance and a kinder understanding, is one main object of our Household Words.

"The mightier inventions of this age are not to our thinking all material, but have a kind of souls in their stupendous bodies which may find expression in Household Words. The traveller whom we accompany on his railroad or his steamboat journey, may gain, we hope, some compensation for incidents which these later generations have outlived, in new associations with the Power that bears him onward; with the habitations and the ways of life of crowds of his fellow-creatures among whom he passes like the wind; even with the towering chimneys he may see, spirting out fire and smoke upon the prospect. The swart giants, slaves of the Lamp of Knowledge, have their thousand and one tales, no less than the genii of the East; and these, in all their wild, grotesque, and fanciful aspects, in all their many phases of endurance, in all their many moving lessons of compassion and consideration, we design to tell.

"Our Household Words will not be echoes of the present time alone, but of the past too. Neither will they treat of the hopes, the enterprises, triumphs, joys and sorrows, of this country only, but, in some degree, of those of every nation upon earth. For nothing can be a source of real interest in one of them, without concerning all the rest.

"We have considered what an ambition it is to be admitted into many homes with affection and confidence; to be regarded as a friend by children and old people; to be thought of in affliction and in happiness; to people the sick room with airy shapes 'that give delight and hurt not,' and to be associated with the harmless laughter and the gentle tears of many hearths. We know the great responsibility of such a privilege; its vast reward; the pictures that it conjures up, in hours of solitary labour, of a multitude moved by one sympathy; the solemn hopes which it awakens in the labourer's breast, that he may be free from self-reproach in looking back at last upon his work, and that his name may be remembered in his race in time to come, and borne by the dear objects of his love with pride. The hand that writes these faltering lines, happily associated with *some* Household Words before to-day, has known enough of such experiences to enter in an earnest spirit upon this new task, and with an awakened sense of all that it involves.

"Some tillers of the field into which we now come, have been before us, and some are here whose high usefulness we readily acknowledge, and whose company it is an honour to join. But, there are others here—Bastards of the Mountain, draggled fringe on the Red Cap, Panders to the basest passions of the lowest natures—whose existence is a national reproach. And these, we should consider it our highest service to displace.

"Thus, we begin our career! The adventurer in the old fairy story, climbing towards the summit of a steep eminence on which the object of his search was stationed, was surrounded by a roar of voices, crying to him, from the stones in the way, to turn back. All the voices *we* hear, cry 'Go on!' The stones that call to us have sermons in them, as the trees have tongues, as there are books in the running brooks, as there is good in everything! They, and the Time, cry out to us 'Go on!' With a fresh heart, a light step, and a hopeful courage, we begin the journey. The road is not so rough that it need daunt our feet: the way is not so steep that we need stop for breath, and, looking faintly down, be stricken motionless. 'Go on,' is all we hear, 'Go on!' In a glow already, with the air from yonder height upon us, and the inspiriting voices joining in this acclamation, we echo back the cry, and go on cheerily."

And so with Mrs. Gaskell's Lizzie Leigh, and a great number of articles was Household Words launched. Dickens' friend, the Reverend J. White, thought the journal highly popular but *expensive*. Wrote Dickens: "It is expensive, no doubt, and demands a large circulation; but it is taking a great and steady stand, and I have no doubt yields a good sound profit."[1]

Dickens, however, was always preoccupied by the great festival of Christmas, and it was the Christmas numbers to which he gave his most considered thoughts. One of the principal features, therefore, of the Christmas

[1] Fitzgerald, *Memories of Charles Dickens*, p. 136.

numbers was the inclusion of a specially written story. In 1851 Dickens met Wilkie Collins, a nervous shy man of very great charm, and a novelist whose popularity and qualities were in certain cases to bear very favourable comparison with the Master. When Dickens met Collins he was engaged upon his famous production of Bulwer-Lytton's *Not as Bad as We Seem*. Among Wilkie Collins' qualities was a love for acting. Wills was asked to play a part in this production but he refused on the grounds that he was too busy, as a result, at Augustus Egg's suggestion, Wilkie Collins was proposed. He played the part admirably, and the play which was in aid of the Guild of Literature and Art and was staged at Devonshire House before the Queen and the Prince Consort was an unqualified success. The friendship between Dickens and Collins was cemented.

The following year Dickens stayed with Collins at Bologne and later in the year, accompanied by Augustus Egg, the three of them went on a tour of Switzerland and Italy. It was that year (1852) that Collins contributed to Household Words one of his last examples of horror stories "A Terribly Strange Bed."

"The Wreck of the Golden Mary" was planned by Dickens and Wilkie Collins in Paris during the winter of 1855-6. Of the three chapters which compose the story, the Wreck itself was written by Dickens—the remainder by Wilkie Collins. The child's verses included in Chapter II caused something of a sensation and Dickens was especially commended for these rather sentimental lines by a Reverend Davis. The girl Lucy who appears in the tale is said to have been based on his friend George Stronghill's sister Lucy, a neighbour at Chatham with whom Dickens was friendly, Lucy being a youthful sweetheart. The story must have been an astounding success since the sale of Household Words reached the phenomenal sale of 100,000 copies. It was published in book form in 1898, *The Wreck of The Golden Mary*, by Charles Dickens and Others.

HERBERT VAN THAL

LONDON, 1955

PART ONE

The Wreck

*Being the Captain's Account of the loss of
the Ship and the Mate's Account of the Great
Deliverance of Her People in an Open Boat
at Sea*

CHAPTER I

I was apprenticed to the sea when I was twelve years old, and I have encountered a great deal of rough weather, both literal and metaphorical. It has always been my opinion since I first possessed such a thing as an opinion, that the man who knows only one subject is next tiresome to the man who knows no subject. Therefore, in the course of my life I have taught myself whatever I could, and although I am not an educated man, I am able, I am thankful to say, to have an intelligent interest in most things.

A person might suppose, from reading the above, that I am in the habit of holding forth about number one. That is not the case. Just as if I was to come into a room among strangers, and must either be introduced or introduce myself, so I have taken the liberty of passing these few remarks, simply and plainly, that it may be known who and what I am. I will add no more of the sort than that my name is William George Ravender, that I was born at Penrith half a year after my own father was drowned, and that I am on the second day of this present blessed Christmas week of one thousand eight hundred and fifty-six, fifty-six years of age.

When the rumour first went flying up and down that there was gold in California—which, as most people know, was before it was discovered in the British colony of Australia—I was in the West Indies, trading among the Islands. Being in command and likewise part-owner of a smart schooner, I had my work cut out for me, and I was doing it. Consequently, gold in California was no business of mine.

But, by the time when I came home to England again, the thing was as clear as your hand held up before you at noonday. There was Californian gold in the museums and in the goldsmiths' shops, and the very first time I went upon 'Change, I met a friend of mine (a seafaring man like myself), with a Californian nugget hanging to his watch-chain. I handled it. It was as like a peeled walnut with bits unevenly broken off here and there, and then electrotyped all over, as ever I saw anything in my life.

I am a single man (she was too good for this world and for me, and she died six weeks before our marriage-day), so when I am ashore, I live in my house at Poplar. My house at Poplar is taken care of and kept ship-shape by an old lady who was my mother's maid before I was born. She is as handsome and as upright as any old lady in the world. She is as fond of me as if she had ever had an only son, and I was he. Well do I know wherever I sail that she never lays down her head at night without having said, "Merciful Lord! bless and preserve William George Ravender, and send him safe home, through Christ our Saviour!" I have thought of it in many a dangerous moment, when it has done me no harm, I am sure.

In my house at Poplar, along with this old lady, I lived quiet for best part of a year, having had a long spell of it among the Islands, and having (which was very uncommon in me), taken the fever rather badly. At last, being strong and hearty, and having read every book I could lay hold of, right out, I was walking down Leadenhall Street in the City of London, thinking of turning-to again, when I met what I call Smithick and Watersby of Liverpool. I chanced to lift up my eyes from looking in at a ship's chronometer in a window, and I saw him bearing down upon me, head on.

It is, personally, neither Smithick, nor Watersby, that I here mention, nor was I ever acquainted with any man of either of those names, nor do I think that there has been anyone of either of those names in that Liverpool House itself that I refer to; and a wiser merchant or a truer gentleman never stepped.

"My dear Captain Ravender," says he. "Of all the men on earth, I wanted to see you most. I was on my way to you."

21

"Well!" says I. "That looks as if you *were* to see me, don't it?" With that, I put my arm in his, and we walked on towards the Royal Exchange, and when we got there, walked up and down at the back of it where the clock-tower is. We walked an hour and more, for he had much to say to me. He had a scheme for chartering a new ship of their own to take out cargo to the diggers and emigrants in California, and to buy and bring back gold. Into the particulars of that scheme I will not enter, and I have no right to enter. All I say of it is that it was a very original one, a very fine one, a very sound one, and a very lucrative one, beyond doubt.

He imparted it to me as freely as if I had been a part of himself. After doing so, he made me the handsomest sharing offer that ever was made to me, boy or man—or I believe to any other captain in the Merchant Navy—and he took this round turn to finish with:

"Ravender, you are well aware that the lawlessness of that coast and country at present is as special as the circumstances in which it is placed. Crews of vessels outward-bound desert as soon as they make the land; crews of vessels homeward-bound ship at enormous wages, with the express intention of murdering the captain and seizing the gold freight; no man can trust another, and the devil seem let loose. Now," says he, "you know my opinion of you, and you know I am only expressing it, and with no singularity, when I tell you that you are almost the only man on whose integrity, discretion and energy——," etc., etc. For, I don't want to repeat what he said, though I was and am sensible of it.

Notwithstanding my being, as I have mentioned, quite

ready for a voyage, still I had some doubts of this voyage. Of course I knew, without being told, that there were peculiar difficulties and dangers in it, a long way over and above those which attend all voyages. It must not be supposed that I was afraid to face them; but, in my opinion a man has no manly motive or sustainment in his own breast for facing dangers, unless he has well considered what they are, and is able quietly to say to himself: "None of these perils can now take me by surprise; I shall know what to do for the best in any of them; all the rest lies in the higher and greater hands to which I humbly commit myself." On this principle I have so attentively considered (regarding it as my duty) all the hazards I have ever been able to think of, in the ordinary way of storm, shipwreck and fire at sea, that I hope should be prepared to do, in any of those cases, whatever could be done, to save the lives entrusted to my charge.

As I was thoughtful, my good friend proposed that he should leave me to walk there as long as I liked, and that I should dine with him by-and-by at his club in Pall Mall. I accepted the invitation, and I walked up and down there, quarter-deck fashion, a matter of a couple of hours; now and then looking up at the weathercock as I might have looked up aloft, and now and then taking a look into Cornhill, as I might have taken a look over the side.

All dinner-time, and all after dinner-time, we talked it over again. I gave him my views of his plan, and he very much approved of the same. I told him I had nearly decided, but not quite. "Well, well," says he, "come down to Liverpool to-morrow with me, and see the

Golden Mary." I liked the name (her name was Mary, and she was golden, if golden stands for good), so I began to feel that it was almost done when I said I would go to Liverpool. On the next morning but one we were on board the *Golden Mary.* I might have known, from his asking me to come down and see her, what she was. I declare her to have been the completest and most exquisite Beauty that I ever set my eyes upon.

We had inspected every timber in her, and had come back to the gangway to go ashore from the dock-basin, when I put out my hand to my friend. "Touch upon it," says I, "and touch heartily. I take command of this ship, and I am hers and yours, if I can get John Steadiman for my chief mate."

John Steadiman had sailed with me four voyages. The first voyage, John was third mate out to China, and came home second. The other three voyages, he was my first officer. At this time of chartering the *Golden Mary,* he was aged thirty-two. A brisk, bright, blue-eyed fellow, a very neat figure and rather under the middle size, never out of the way and never in it, a face that pleased everybody and that all children took to, a habit of going about singing as cheerily as a blackbird, and a perfect sailor.

We were in one of those Liverpool hackney-coaches in less than a minute, and we cruised about in her upwards of three hours, looking for John. John had come home from Van Diemen's Land barely a month before, and I had heard of him as taking a frisk in Liverpool. We asked after him, among many other places, at the two boarding-houses he was fondest of, and we found he had had a week's spell at each of them; but, he had gone here and gone there, and had set off "to lay out on the main-to'-gallant-yard of the highest Welsh mountain" (so he had told the people of the house), and where he might be then, or when he might come back nobody could tell us. But it was surprising, to be sure, to see how every face brightened the moment there was mention made of the name of Mr. Steadiman.

We were taken aback at meeting with no better luck, and we had wore ship and put her head for my friends, when, as we were jogging through the streets, I clap my eyes on John himself coming out of a toy-shop! He was carrying a little boy, and conducting two uncommon pretty women to their coach; and he told me afterwards that he had never in his life seen one of the three before, but that he was so taken with them on looking in at the toy-shop while they were buying the child a cranky Noah's Ark, very much down by the head, that he had gone in and asked the ladies' permission to treat him to a tolerably correct Cutter there in the window, in order that such a handsome boy might not grow up with a lubberly idea of naval architecture.

We stood off and on until the ladies' coachman began to give way, and then we hailed John. On his coming aboard of us, I told him, very gravely, what I had said to my friend. It struck him, as he said himself, amidships. He was quite shaken by it. "Captain Ravender," were John Steadiman's words, "such an opinion from you is true commendation, and I'll sail round the world with you for twenty years if you hoist the signal, and stand by you for ever!" And now, indeed, I felt that it was done, and that the *Golden Mary* was afloat.

Grass never yet grew under the feet of Smithick and Watersby. The riggers were out of that ship in a fortnight's time, and we had begun taking in cargo. John was always aboard, seeing everything stowed with his own eyes; and whenever I went aboard myself, early or late, whether he was below in the hold, or on deck at the hatchway, or overhauling his cabin, nailing up pictures in it of the Blush Roses of England, the Blue Belles of Scotland, and the female Shamrock of Ireland; of a certainty I heard John singing like a blackbird.

We had room for twenty passengers. Our sailing advertisement was no sooner out, than we might have taken these, twenty times over. In entering our men, I and John (both together) picked them, and we entered none but good hands—as good as were to be found in that port. And so, in a good ship of the best build, well owned, well arranged, well officered, well manned, well founded in all respects, we parted with our pilot at a quarter past four o'clock in the afternoon of the seventh of March, one thousand eight hundred and fifty-one, and stood with a fair wind out to sea.

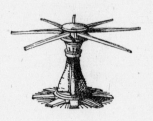

CHAPTER II

IT may be easily believed that up to that time I had had no leisure to be intimate with my passengers. The most of them were then in their berths sea-sick; however in going among them, telling them what was good for them, persuading them not to be there, but to come up on deck and feel the breeze, and in rousing them with a joke, or a comfortable word, I made acquaintance with them, perhaps in a more friendly and confidential way from the first, than I might have done at the cabin table.

Of my passengers, I need only particularize, just at present, a bright-eyed, blooming young wife who was going out to join her husband in California, taking with her their only child, a little girl of three years old, whom he had never seen; a sedate young woman in black, some five years older (about thirty, as I should say), who was going out to join a brother; and an old gentleman, a good deal like a hawk if his eyes had been better and not so red, who was always talking, morning, noon and night, about the gold discovery. But, whether he was making the voyage, thinking his old arms could dig for gold, or whether his speculation was to buy it, or to barter for it, or to cheat for it, or to snatch it anyhow from other people, was his secret. He kept his secret.

These three and the child were the soonest well. The child was a most engaging child, to be sure, and very fond of me; though I am bound to admit that John Steadiman and I were borne on her pretty little books in reverse order, and that he was captain there, and I was mate. It was beautiful to watch her with John, and it was beautiful to watch John with her. Few would have thought it possible, to see John playing at bo-peep round the mast, that he was the man who had caught up an iron bar and struck a Malay and a Maltese dead, as they were gliding with their knives down the cabin stair aboard the barque *Old England*, when the captain lay ill in his cot, off Saugar Point. But he was; and give him his back against a bulwark, he would have done the same by half a dozen of them. The name of the young mother was Mrs. Atherfield, the name of the young lady in black was Miss Coleshaw, and the name of the old gentleman was Mr. Rarx.

As the child had a quantity of shining fair hair,

clustering in curls all about her face, and as her name was Lucy, Steadiman gave her the name of the Golden Lucy. So, we had the Golden Lucy and the *Golden Mary*; and John kept up the idea to that extent as he and the child went playing about the decks, that I believe she used to think the ship was alive somehow—a sister or companion, going to the same place as herself. She liked to be by the wheel, and in fine weather, I have often stood by the man whose trick it was at the wheel, only to hear her, sitting near my feet, talking to the ship. Never had a child such a doll before, I suppose; but she made a doll of the *Golden Mary*, and used to dress her up by tying ribbons and little bits of finery to the belaying-pins; and nobody ever moved them, unless it was to save them from being blown away.

Of course, I took charge of the two young women, and I called them "my dear," and they never minded, knowing that whatever I said was said in a fatherly and protecting spirit. I gave them their places on each side of me at dinner, Mrs. Atherfield on my right and Miss Coleshaw on my left; and I directed the unmarried lady to serve out the tea. Likewise, I said to my black steward in their presence: "Tom Snow, these two ladies are equally the mistresses of this house, and do you obey their orders equally." At which Tom laughed, and they all laughed.

Old Mr. Rarx was not a pleasant man to look at, nor yet to talk to, or to be with, for no one could help seeing that he was a sordid and selfish character, and that he had warped further and further out of the straight with time. Not but what he was on his best behaviour with us, as everybody was; for, we had no bickering among us, for'ard or aft. I only mean to say, he was not the man one would have chosen for a messmate. If choice there had been, one might even have gone a few points out of one's course, to say, "No! Not him!" But, there was one curious inconsistency in Mr. Rarx. That was, that he took an astonishing interest in the child. He looked, and, I may add, he was, one of the last of men to care at all for a child, or to care much for any human creature. Still, he went so far as to be habitually uneasy, if the child was long on deck, out of his sight. He was always afraid of her falling overboard, or falling down a hatchway, or of a block or whatnot coming down upon her from the rigging in the working of the ship, or of her getting some hurt or other. He used to look at her and touch her as if she was something precious to him. He was always solicitous about her not injuring her health, and constantly entreated her mother to be careful of it. This was so much the more curious, because the child did not like him, but used to shrink away from him, and would not even put out her hand to him without coaxing from others. I believe that every soul on board frequently noticed this, and that not one of us understood it. However, it was such a plain fact, that John Steadiman said more than once when old Mr. Rarx was not within earshot, that if the *Golden Mary* felt a tenderness for the dear old gentleman she carried in her lap, she must be bitterly jealous of the Golden Lucy.

Before I go any further with this narrative, I will state that our ship was a barque of three hundred tons, carrying a crew of eighteen men, a second mate in

30

addition to John, a carpenter, an armourer or smith, and two apprentices (one a Scotch boy, poor little fellow). We had three boats—the Long-boat, capable of carrying twenty-five men; the Cutter, capable of carrying fifteen; and the Surf-boat, capable of carrying ten. I put down the capacity of these boats according to the numbers they were really meant to hold.

We had tastes of bad weather and head-winds, of course; but on the whole we had as fine a run as any reasonable man could expect, for sixty days. I then began to enter two remarks in the ship's Log and in my Journal. First, that there was an unusual and amazing quantity of ice; second, that the nights were most wonderfully dark, in spite of the ice.

For five days and a half, it seemed quite useless and hopeless to alter the ship's course so as to stand out of the way of this ice. I made what southing I could; but all that time, we were beset by it. Mrs. Atherfield, after standing by me on deck once, looking for some time in an awed manner at the great bergs that surrounded us, said in a whisper, "O! Captain Ravender, it looks as if the whole solid earth had changed into ice and broken up!" I said to her, laughing, "I don't wonder that it does, to your inexperienced eyes, my dear." But I had never seen a twentieth part of the quantity, and, in reality, I was pretty much of her opinion.

However, at two p.m. on the afternoon of the sixth day, that is to say, when we were sixty-six days out, John Steadiman, who had gone aloft, sang out from the top that the sea was clear ahead. Before four p.m., a strong breeze springing up right astern, we were in open water at sunset. The breeze then freshening into half a gale of wind, and the *Golden Mary* being a very fast sailer, we went before the wind merrily, all night.

I had thought it impossible that it could be darker than it had been, until the sun, moon and stars should fall out of the Heavens, and Time should be destroyed; but it had been next to light, in comparison with what it was now. The darkness was so profound, that looking into it was painful and oppressive—like looking, without a ray of light, into a dense black bandage put as close before the eyes as it could be, without touching them. I doubled the look-out, and John and I stood in the bow side by side, never leaving it all night. Yet I should no more have known that he was near me when he was silent, without putting out my arm and touching him, than I should if he had turned in and been fast asleep below. We were not so much looking out, all of us, as listening to the utmost, both with our eyes and ears.

Next day I found that the mercury in the barometer, which had risen steadily since we cleared the ice, remained steady. I had had very good observations, with now and then the interruption of a day or so, since our departure. I got the sun at noon, and found that we were in Lat. 58°S., Long. 60°W., off New South Shetland, in the neighbourhood of Cape Horn. We were sixty-seven days out, that day. The ship's reckoning was accurately worked and made up. The ship did her duty admirably, all on board were well, and all hands were as smart, efficient and contented, as it was possible to be.

When the night came on again as dark as before, it was

the eighth night I had been on deck. Nor had I taken more than a very little sleep in the day-time, my station being always near the helm, and often at it, while we were among the ice. Few but those who have tried it can imagine the difficulty and pain of only keeping the eyes open—physically open—under such circumstances, in such darkness. They get struck by the darkness, and blinded by the darkness. They make patterns in it, and they flash in it, as if they had gone out of your head to look at you. On the turn of midnight, John Steadiman, who was alert and fresh (for I had always made him turn in by day), said to me, "Captain Ravender, I entreat of you to go below. I am sure you can hardly stand, and your voice is getting weak, sir. Go below, and take a little rest. I'll call you if a block chafes." I said to John in answer, "Well, well, John! Let us wait till the turn of one o'clock, before we talk about that." I had just had one of the ship's lanterns held up, that I might see how the night went by my watch, and it was then twenty minutes after twelve.

At five minutes before one, John sang out to the boy to bring the lantern again, and, when I told him once more what the time was, entreated and prayed of me to go below. "Captain Ravender," says he, "all's well; we can't afford to have you laid up for a single hour; and I respectfully and earnestly beg of you to go below." The end of it was that I agreed to do so, on the understanding that if I failed to come up of my own accord within three hours, I was to be punctually called. Having settled that, I left John in charge. But, I called him to me once afterwards, to ask him a question. I had been to look at the barometer, and had seen the mercury still perfectly steady, and had come up the companion again, to take a last look about me—if I can use such a word in reference to such darkness—when I thought that the waves, as the *Golden Mary* parted them and shook them off, had a hollow sound in them; something that I fancied was a rather unusual reverberation. I was standing by the quarter-deck rail on the starboard side, when I called John aft to me, and bade him listen. He did so with the greatest attention. Turning to me he then said, "Rely upon it, Captain Ravender, you have been without rest too long, and the novelty is only in the state of your sense of hearing." I thought so, too, by that time, and I think so now, though I can never know for absolute certain this world, whether it was or not.

When I left John Steadiman in charge, the ship was still going at a great rate through the water. The wind still blew right astern. Though she was making great way, she was under shortened sail, and had no more than she could easily carry. All was snug, and nothing complained. There was a pretty sea running, but not a very high sea neither, nor at all a confused one.

I turned in, as we seamen say, all standing. The meaning of that is, I did not pull my clothes off—no, not even so much as my coat; though I did my shoes, for my feet were badly swelled with the deck. There was a little swing-lamp alight in my cabin. I thought, as I looked at it before shutting my eyes, that I was so tired of darkness, and troubled by darkness, that I could have gone to sleep best in the midst of a million of flaming gas-lights. That was the last thought I had before I went off, except the prevailing thought that I should not be able to get to sleep at all.

I dreamed that I was back at Penrith again, and was trying to get round the church, which had altered its shape very much since I last saw it, and was cloven all down the middle of the steeple in a most singular manner. Why I wanted to get round the church, I don't know; but I was as anxious to do it as if my life depended on it. Indeed, I believe it did, in the dream. For all that, I could not get round the church. I was still trying, when I came against it with a violent shock, and was flung out of my cot against the ship's side. Shrieks and a terrific outcry struck me far harder than the bruising timbers, and amidst sounds of grinding and crashing, and a heavy rushing and breaking of water—sounds I understood too well—I made my way on deck. It was not an easy thing to do, for the ship heeled over frightfully, and was beating in a furious manner.

I could not see the men as I went forward, but I could hear that they were hauling in sail, in disorder. I had my trumpet in my hand, and after directing and encouraging them in this till it was done, I hailed first John Steadiman, and then my second mate, Mr. William Rames. Both answered clearly and steadily. Now, I had practised them and all my crew, as I have ever made it a custom to practise all who sail with me, to take certain stations, and wait my orders, in case of any unexpected crisis. When my voice was heard hailing, and their voices were heard answering, I was aware, through all the noises of the ship and sea, and all the crying of the passengers below, that there was a pause. "Are you ready, Rames?" "Aye,

aye, sir!" "Then light up, for God's sake!" In a moment he and another were burning blue-lights, and the ship and all on board seemed to be enclosed in a mist of light, under a great black dome.

The light shone up so high that I could see the huge iceberg upon which we had struck, cloven at the top and down the middle, exactly like Penrith Church in my dream. At the same moment I could see the watch last relieved, crowding up and down on deck; I could see Mrs. Atherfield and Miss Coleshaw thrown about on the top of the companion as they struggled to bring the child up from below; I could see that the masts were going with the shock and the beating of the ship; I could see the frightful breach stove in on the starboard side, half the length of the vessel, and the sheathing and timbers spurting up; I could see that the Cutter was disabled, in a wreck of broken fragments; and I could see every eye turned upon me. It is my belief that if there had been ten thousand eyes there, I should have seen them all, with their different looks. And all this in a moment. But you must consider what a moment.

I saw the men, as they looked at me, fall towards their appointed stations, like good men and true. If she had not righted, they could have done very little there or anywhere but die—not that it is little for a man to die at his post. I mean they could have done nothing to save the passengers and themselves. Happily, however, the violence of the shock with which we had so determinedly borne down direct on that fatal iceberg, as if it had been our destination instead of our destruction, had so smashed and pounded the ship that she got off in this same instant, and righted. I did not want the carpenter to tell me she was filling and going down; I could see and hear that. I gave Rames the word to lower the Long-boat and the Surf-boat, and I myself told off the men for each duty. Not one hung back, or came before the other. I now whispered to John Steadiman, "John, I stand at the gangway here, to see every soul on board safe over the side. You shall have the next post of honour, and shall be the last but one to leave the ship. Bring up the passengers, and range them behind me; and put what provision and water you can get at in the boats. Cast your eye for'ard, John and you'll see you have not a moment to lose."

My noble fellows got the boats over the side as orderly as I ever saw boats lowered with any sea running, and when they were launched, two or three of the nearest men in them as they held on, rising and falling with the swell, called out, looking up at me, "Captain Ravender, if any thing goes wrong with us and you are saved, remember we stood by you!" "We'll all stand by one another ashore, yet, please God, my lads!" says I. "Hold on bravely, and be tender with the women."

The women were an example to us. They trembled very much, but they were quiet and perfectly collected. "Kiss me, Captain Ravender," says Mrs. Atherfield, "and God in Heaven bless you, you good man!" "My dear," says I, "those words are better for me than a life-boat." I held her child in my arms till she was in the boat, and then kissed the child and handed her safe down. I now said to the people in her, "You have got your freight my lads, all but me, and I'm not coming yet awhile. Pull away from the ship, and keep off!"

That was the Long-boat. Old Mr. Rarx was one of her complement, and he was the only passenger who had greatly misbehaved since the ship struck. Others had been a little wild, which was not to be wondered at, and not very blameable; but he had made a lamentation and uproar which it was dangerous for the people to hear, as there is always contagion in weakness and selfishness. His incessant cry had been that he must not be separated from the child, that he couldn't see the child, and that he and the child must go together. He had even tried to wrest the child out of my arms, that he might keep her in his. "Mr. Rarx," said I to him when it came to that, "I have a loaded pistol in my pocket, and if you don't stand out of the gangway, and keep perfectly quiet, I shall shoot you through the heart, if you have got one." Says he, "You won't do murder, Captain Ravender?" "No, sir," says I, "I won't murder forty-four people to humour you, but I'll shoot you to save them." After that, he was quiet, and stood shivering a little way off, until I named him to go over the side.

The Long-boat being cast off, the Surf-boat was soon filled. There only remained aboard the *Golden Mary*, John Mullion, the man who had kept on burning the blue-lights (and who had lighted every new one at every old one before it went out, as quietly as if he had been at an illumination); John Steadiman; and myself. I hurried those two into the Surf-boat, called to them to keep off, and waited with a grateful and relieved heart for the Long-boat to come and take me in, if she could. I looked at my watch, and it showed me, by the blue-light, ten minutes past two. They lost no time. As soon as she was near enough, I swung myself into her, and called to the men, "With a will, lads! She's reeling!" We were not an inch too far out of the inner vortex of her going down when, by the blue-light which John Mullion still burnt in the bow of the Surf-boat, we saw her lurch, and plunge to the bottom head-foremost. The child cried, weeping wildly, "O, the dear *Golden Mary!* O, look at her! Save her! Save the poor *Golden Mary!*" And then the light burnt out, and the black dome seemed to come down upon us.

I suppose if we had all stood a-top of a mountain, and seen the whole remainder of the world sink away from under us, we could hardly have felt more shocked and solitary than we did when we knew we were alone on the wide ocean, and that the beautiful ship in which most of us had been securely asleep within half an hour was gone for ever. There was an awful silence in our boat, and such a kind of palsy on the rowers and the man at the rudder, that I felt they were scarcely keeping her before the sea. I spoke out then, and said, "Let everyone here thank the Lord for our preservation!" All the voices answered (even the child's), "We thank the Lord!" I then said the Lord's Prayer, and all hands said it after me with a solemn murmuring. Then I gave the word "Cheerily, O men, cheerily!" and I felt that they were handling the boat again as a boat ought to be handled.

The Surf-boat now burnt another blue-light to show us where they were, and we made for her, and laid ourselves as nearly alongside of her as we dared. I had always kept my boats with a coil or two of good stout stuff in each of them, so both boats had a rope at hand. We made a shift, with much labour and trouble, to get near enough to one another to divide the blue-lights (they were no use after that night, for the sea water soon got at them), and to get a tow-rope out between us. All night long we kept together, sometimes obliged to cast off the rope, and sometimes getting it out again, and all of us wearying for the morning—which appeared so long in coming that old Mr. Rarx screamed out, in spite of his fears of me, "The world is drawing to an end, and the sun will never rise any more!"

CHAPTER III

WHEN the day broke, I found that we were all
huddled together in a miserable manner. We
were deep in the water, being, as I found on
mustering, thirty-one in number, being at least four
too many. The first thing I did was to get myself passed
to the rudder—which I took from that time—and to
get Mrs. Atherfield, her child, and Miss Coleshaw,
passed on to sit next me. As to old Mr. Rarx, I put
him in the bow, as far from us as I could. And I put
some of the best men near us, in order that if I should

drop, there might be a skilful hand ready to take the helm.

The sea moderating as the sun came up, though the sky was cloudy and wild, we spoke to the other boat to know what stores they had, and to overhaul what we had. I had a compass in my pocket, a small telescope, a double-barrelled pistol, a knife, and a fire-box and matches. Most of my men had knives, and some had a little tobacco; some, a pipe as well. We had a mug among us, and an iron-spoon. As to provisions, there were in my boat two bags of biscuits, one piece of raw beef, one piece of raw pork, a bag of coffee, roasted but not ground (thrown in, I imagine, by mistake, for something else), two small casks of water, and about half a gallon of rum in a keg. The Surf-boat, having rather more rum than we, and fewer to drink it, gave us, as I estimated, another quart into our keg. In return, we gave them a piece of handkerchief. They reported that they had aboard, besides, a bag of biscuits, a piece of beef, a small cask of water, a small box of lemons, and a Dutch cheese. It took a long time to make these exchanges, and they were not made without risk to both parties, the sea running quite high enough to make our approaching near to one another very hazardous. In the bundle with the coffee, I conveyed to John Steadiman (who had a ship's compass with him), a paper written in pencil, and torn from my pocket-book, containing the course I meant to steer, in the hope of making land or being picked up by some vessel—I say in the hope, though I had little hope of either deliverance. I then sang out to him, so as all might hear, that if we two boats could

42

live or die together, we would; but, that if we should be parted by the weather, and join company no more, they should have our prayers and blessings, and we asked for theirs. We then gave them three cheers, which they returned, and I saw the men's heads droop in both boats as they fell to their oars again.

These arrangements had occupied the general attention advantageously for all, though (as I expressed in the last sentence) they ended in a sorrowful feeling. I now said a few words to my fellow-voyagers on the subject of the small stock of food on which our lives depended if they were preserved from the great deep, and on the rigid necessity of our eking it out in the most frugal manner. One and all replied that whatever allowance I thought best to lay down should be strictly kept to. We made a pair of scales out of a thin scrap of iron-plating and some twine, and I got together for weights such of the heaviest buttons among us as I calculated made up some fraction over two ounces. This was the allowance of solid food served out once a day to each, from that time to the end, with the addition of a coffee berry, or sometimes half a one, when the weather was very fair, for breakfast. We had nothing else whatever but half a pint of water each per day, and sometimes, when we were coldest and weakest, a teaspoonful of rum each, served out as a dram. I know how learnedly it can be shown that rum is poison, but I also know that in this case, as in all similar cases I have ever read of—which are numerous—no words can express the comfort and support derived from it. Nor have I the least doubt that it saved the lives of far more than half our number. Having mentioned half a pint

43

of water as our daily allowance, I ought to observe that sometimes we had less, and sometimes we had more; for, much rain fell, and we caught it in a canvas stretched for the purpose.

Thus, at that tempestuous time of the year, and in that tempestuous part of the world, we shipwrecked people rose and fell with the waves. It is not my intention to relate (if I can avoid it) such circumstances appertaining to our doleful condition as have been better told in many other narratives of the kind than I can be expected to tell them. I will only note, in so many passing words, that day after day, and night after night, we received the sea upon our backs to prevent it from swamping the boat; that one party was always kept baling, and that every hat and cap among us soon got worn out, though patched up fifty times, as the only vessels we had for that service; that another party lay down in the bottom of the boat, while a third rowed; and that we were soon all in boils and blisters and rags.

The other boat was a source of such anxious interest to all of us that I used to wonder whether, if we were saved, the time could ever come when the survivors in this boat of ours could be at all indifferent to the fortunes of the survivors in that. We got out a tow-rope whenever the weather permitted, but that did not often happen, and how we two parties kept within the same horizon as we did. He, who mercifully permitted it to be so for our consolation, only knows. I never shall forget the looks with which, when the morning light came, we used to gaze about us over the stormy waters for the other boat. We once parted company for seventy-two hours, and we believed them to have gone down, as they did us. The joy on both sides, when we came within view of one another again, had something in a manner Divine in it; each was so forgetful of individual suffering, in tears of delight and sympathy for the people in the other boat.

I have been wanting to get round to the individual or personal part of my subject, as I call it, and the foregoing incident puts me in the right way. The patience and good disposition aboard of us was wonderful. I was not surprised by it in the women, for all men born of women know what great qualities they will show when men will fail; but I own I was a little surprised by it in some of the men. Among one-and-thirty people assembled at the best of times, there will usually, I should say, be two or three uncertain tempers. I knew that I had more than one rough temper with me among my own people, for I had chosen those for the Long-boat that I might have them under my eye. But they softened under their misery, and were as considerate of the ladies, and as compassionate of the child, as the best among us, or among men—they could not have been more so. I heard scarcely any complaining. The party lying down would moan a good deal in their sleep, and I would often notice a man—not always the same man, it is to be understood, but nearly all of them at one time or other—sitting moaning at his oar, or in his place, as he looked mistily over the sea. When it happened to be long before I could catch his eye, he would go on moaning all the time in the dismallest manner; but, when our looks met, he would brighten and leave off. I almost got the impression that he did not know what sound he had been making, but that he thought he had been humming a tune.

Our sufferings from cold and wet were far greater than our sufferings from hunger. We managed to keep the child warm, but I doubt if anyone else among us ever was warm for five minutes together, and the shivering and the chattering of teeth were sad to hear. The child cried a little at first for her lost playfellow, the *Golden Mary*, but hardly ever whimpered afterwards; and when the state of the weather made it possible, she used now and then to be held up in the arms of some of us, to look over the sea for John Steadiman's boat. I see the golden hair and the innocent face now, between me and the driving clouds, like an Angel going to fly away.

It had happened on the second day, towards night, that Mrs. Atherfield, in getting little Lucy to sleep, sang her a song. She had a soft, melodious voice, and when she had finished it, our people up and begged for another. She sang them another, and after it had fallen dark ended with the Evening Hymn. From that time, whenever anything could be heard above the sea and wind, and while she had any voice left, nothing would serve the people but that she should sing at sunset. She always did, and always ended with the Evening Hymn. We mostly took up the last line, and shed tears when it was done, but not miserably. We had a prayer night and morning also, when the weather allowed of it.

Twelve nights and eleven days we had been driving in the boat, when old Mr. Rarx began to be delirious and to cry out to me to throw the gold overboard or it would sink us, and we should all be lost. For days past

46

the child had been declining, and that was the great cause of his wildness. He had been over and over again shrieking out to me to give her all the remaining meat, to give her all the remaining rum, to save her at any cost, or we should all be ruined. At this time, she lay in her mother's arms at my feet. One of her little hands was almost always creeping about her mother's neck or chin. I had watched the wasting of the little hand, and I knew it was nearly over.

The old man's cries were so discordant with the mother's love and submission, that I called out to him in an angry voice, unless he held his peace on the instant, I would order him to be knocked on the head and thrown overboard. He was mute then until the child died, very peacefully, an hour afterwards, which was known to all in the boat by the mother's breaking out into lamentations for the first time since the wreck— for she had great fortitude and constancy, though she was a little gentle woman. Old Mr. Rarx then became quite ungovernable, tearing what rags he had on him, raging in imprecations, and calling to me that if I had thrown the gold overboard (always the gold with him!) I might have saved the child. "And now," says he, in a terrible voice, "we shall founder, and all go to the Devil, for our sins will sink us, when we have no innocent child to bear us up!" We so discovered with amazement that this old wretch had only cared for the life of the pretty little creature dear to all of us, because of the influence he superstitiously hoped she might have in preserving him! Altogether it was too much for the smith or armourer, who was sitting next the old man, to bear. He took him by the throat and rolled him under the thwarts, where he lay still enough for hours afterwards.

All that thirteenth night Miss Coleshaw, lying across my knees as I kept the helm, comforted and supported the poor mother. Her child, covered with a pea-jacket of mine, lay in her lap. It troubled me all night to think that there was no Prayer Book among us, and that I could remember but very few of the exact words of the burial service. When I stood up at broad day, all knew what was going to be done, and I noticed that my poor fellows made the motion of uncovering their heads, though their heads had been stark bare to the sky and sea for many a weary hour. There was a long heavy swell on, but otherwise it was a fair morning, and there were broad fields of sunlight on the waves in the east. I said no more than this: "I am the Resurrection and the Life, saith the Lord. He raised the daughter of Jairus the ruler, and said she was not dead, but slept. He raised the widow's son. He arose himself, and was seen of many. He loved little children, saying, Suffer them to come unto me and rebuke them not, for of such is the kingdom of Heaven. In his name, my friends, and committed to His merciful goodness!" With those words I laid my rough face softly on the placid little forehead, and buried the Golden Lucy in the grave of the *Golden Mary*.

Having had it on my mind to relate the end of this dear little child, I have omitted something from its exact place, which I will supply here. It will come quite as well here as anywhere else.

Foreseeing that if the boat lived through the stormy

weather the time must come, and soon come, when we should have absolutely no morsel to eat, I had one momentous point often in my thoughts. Although I had, years before that, fully satisfied myself that the instances in which human beings in the last distress have fed upon each other are exceedingly few, and have very seldom indeed (if ever) occurred when the people in distress, however dreadful their extremity, have been accustomed to moderate forbearance and restraint—I say, though I had, long before, quite satisfied my mind on this topic, I felt doubtful whether there might not have been in former cases some harm and danger from keeping it out of sight and pretending not to think of it. I felt doubtful whether some minds, growing weak with fasting and exposure, and having such a terrific idea to dwell upon in secret, might not magnify it until it got to have an awful attraction about it. This was not a new thought of mine, for it had grown out of my reading. However, it came over me stronger than it had ever done before—as it had reason for doing—in the boat, and on the fourth day I decided that I would bring out into the light that uniformed fear which must have been more or less darkly in every brain among us. Therefore, as a means of beguiling the time and inspiring hope, I gave them the best summary in my power of Bligh's voyage of more than three thousand miles, in an open boat, after the Mutiny of the *Bounty*, and of the wonderful preservation of that boat's crew. They listened throughout with great interest, and I concluded by telling them that, in my opinion, the happiest circumstances in the whole narrative was that Bligh, who was no delicate man either, had solemnly placed it on record therein that he was sure and certain that under no conceivable circumstances whatever would that emaciated party, who had gone through all the pains of famine, have preyed on one another. I cannot describe the visible relief which this spread through the boat, and how the tears stood in every eye. From that time I was as well convinced as Bligh himself that there was no danger and that this phantom, at any rate, did not haunt us.

Now, it was a part of Bligh's experience that when the people in his boat were most cast down, nothing did them so much good as hearing a story told by one of their number. When I mentioned that, I saw that it struck the general attention as much as it did my own, for I had not thought of it until I came to it in my summary. This was on the day after Mrs. Atherfield first sang to us. I proposed that whenever the weather would permit, we should have a story two hours after dinner (I always issued the allowance I have mentioned at one o'clock, and called it by that name), as well as our song at sunset. The proposal was received with a cheerful satisfaction that warmed my heart within me; and I do not say too much when I say that those two periods in the four-and-twenty hours were expected with positive pleasure, and were really enjoyed, by all hands. Spectres as we soon were in our bodily wasting, our imaginations did not perish like the gross flesh upon our bones. Music and adventure, two of the great gifts of Providence to mankind, could charm us long after that was lost.

The wind was almost always against us after the second day, and for many days together we could not nearly hold our own. We had all varieties of bad weather. We had rain, hail, snow, wind, mist, thunder and lightning. Still the boats lived through the heavy seas, and still we perishing people rose and fell with the great waves.

Sixteen nights and fifteen days, twenty nights and nineteen days. So the time went on. Disheartening as I knew that our progress, or want of progress, must be, I never deceived them as to my calculations of it. In the first place, I felt that we were all too near eternity for deceit; in the second place, I knew that if I failed, or died, the man who followed me must have a knowledge of the true state of things to begin upon. When I told them at noon what I reckoned we had made or lost, they generally received what I said in a tranquil and resigned manner, and always gratefully towards me. It was not unusual at any time of the day for someone to burst out weeping loudly without any new cause and, when the burst was over, to calm down a little better than before. I had seen exactly the same thing in a house of mourning.

During the whole of this time old Mr. Rarx had had his fits of calling out to me to throw the gold (always the gold!) overboard, and of heaping violent reproaches upon me fot not having saved the child; but now, the food being all but gone, and I having nothing left to serve out but a bit of coffee berry now and then, he began to be too weak to do this, and consequently fell silent. Mrs. Atherfield and Miss Coleshaw generally lay, each with an arm across one of my knees, and her head upon it. They never complained at all. Up to the time of her child's death, Mrs. Atherfield had bound up her own beautiful hair every day; and I took particular notice that this was always before she sang her song at night, when everyone looked at her. But she never did it after the loss of her darling; and it would have been now all tangled with dirt and wet, but that Miss Coleshaw was careful of it long after she was herself, and would sometimes smooth it down with her weak thin hands.

We were past mustering a story now; but one day, at about this period, I reverted to the superstition of old Mr. Rarx, concerning the Golden Lucy, and told them that nothing vanished from the eye of God, though much might pass away from the eyes of men. "We were all of us," says I, "children once, and our baby feet have strolled in green woods ashore, and our baby hands have gathered flowers in gardens, where the birds were singing. The children that we were, are not lost to the great knowledge of our Creator. Those innocent creatures will appear with us before Him, and plead for us. What we were in the best time of our generous youth will arise and go with us, too. The purest part of our lives will not desert us at the pass to which all of us here present are gliding. What we were then, will be as much in existence before Him, as what we are now." They were no less comforted by this consideration than I was myself; and Miss Coleshaw, drawing my ear nearer to her lips, said, "Captain Ravender, I was on my way to marry a disgraced and broken man, whom I dearly loved when he was honourable and good. Your words seem to have come out of my own poor heart." She pressed my hand upon it, smiling.

Twenty-seven nights and twenty-six days. We were in no want of rain-water, but we had nothing else. And yet, even now, I never turned my eyes upon a waking face but it tried to brighten before mine. O! what a thing it is, in a time of danger, and in the presence of death, the shining of a face upon a face! I have heard it broached that orders should be given in great new ships by electric telegraph. I admire machinery as much as any man, and am as thankful to it as any man can be for what it does for us. But it will never be a substitute for the face of a man, with his soul in it, encouraging another man to be brave and true. Never try it for that. It will break down like a straw.

I now began to remark certain changes in myself which I did not like. They caused me much disquiet. I often saw the Golden Lucy in the air above the boat. I often saw her I have spoken of before, sitting beside me. I saw the *Golden Mary* go down as she really had gone down, twenty times in a day. And yet the sea was mostly, to my thinking, not sea neither, but moving country and extraordinary mountainous regions, the like of which have never been beheld. I felt it time to leave my last words regarding John Steadiman, in case any lips should last out to repeat them to any living ears. I said that John had told me (as he had on deck) that he had sung out "Breakers ahead!" the instant they were audible, and had tried to wear ship, but she struck before it could be done. (His cry, I dare say, had made my dream.) I said that the circumstances were altogether without warning and out of any course that could have been guarded against; that the same loss would have happened if I had been in charge; and that John was not to blame, but from first to last had done his duty nobly, like the man he was. I tried to write it down in my pocket-book, but could make no words, though I knew what the words were that I wanted to make. When it had come to that, her hands—though she was dead so long—laid me down gently in the bottom of the boat, and she and the Golden Lucy swung me to sleep.

John Dugan

CHAPTER IV

*All that follows was written by
John Steadiman, Chief Mate*

ON the twenty-sixth day after the foundering of
the *Golden Mary* at sea, I, John Steadiman, was
sitting in my place in the stern-sheets of the Surf-
boat, with just sense enough left in me to steer—that is
to say, with my eyes strained, wide awake, over the
bows of the boat, and my brains fast asleep and dreaming
—when I was roused upon a sudden by our second mate,
Mr. William Rames.

"Let me take a spell in your place," says he. "And look you out for the Long-boat, astern. The last time she rose on the crest of a wave, I thought I made out a signal flying aboard her."

We shifted our places, clumsily and slowly enough, for we were both of us weak and dazed with wet, cold and hunger. I waited some time, watching the heavy rollers astern, before the Long-boat rose a-top of one of them at the same time with us. At last she was heaved up for a moment well in view, and there, sure enough, was the signal flying aboard of her—a strip of rag of some sort, rigged to an oar, and hoisted in her bows.

"What does it mean?" says Rames to me in a quavering, trembling sort of voice. "Do they signal a sail in sight?"

"Hush, for God's sake!" says I, clapping my hand over his mouth. "Don't let the people hear you. They'll all go mad together if we mislead them about that signal. Wait a bit, till I have another look at it."

I held on by him, for he had set me all of a tremble with his notion of a sail in sight, and watched for the Long-boat again. Up she rose on the top of another roller. I made out the signal clearly, that second time, and saw that it was rigged half-mast high.

"Rames," says I, "it's a signal of distress. Pass the word forward to keep her before the sea, and no more. We must get the Long-boat within hailing distance of us as soon as possible."

I dropped down into my old place at the tiller without another word—for the thought went through me like a knife that something had happened to Captain Ravender.

I should consider myself unworthy to write another line
of this statement if I had not made up my mind to speak
the truth, the whole truth, and nothing but the truth—
and I must, therefore, confess plainly that now, for the
first time, my heart sank within me. This weakness on
my part was produced in some degree, as I take it, by
the exhausting effects of previous anxiety and grief.

Our provisions—if I may give that name to what we
had left—were reduced to the rind of one lemon and
about a couple of handfuls of coffee berries. Besides
these great distresses, caused by the death, the danger,
and the suffering among my crew and passengers, I had
had a little distress of my own to shake me still more,
in the death of the child whom I had got to be very fond
of on the voyage out—so fond that I was secretly a
little jealous of her being taken in the Long-boat instead
of mine when the ship foundered. It used to be a great
comfort to me, and I think to those with me also, after
we had seen the last of the *Golden Mary*, to see the Golden
Lucy held up by the men in the Long-boat, when the
weather allowed it, as the best and brightest sight they
had to show. She looked, at the distance we saw her
from, almost like a little white bird in the air. To miss
her for the first time, when the weather lulled a little
again, and we all looked out for our white bird and
looked in vain, was a sore disappointment. To see the
men's heads bowed down and the captain's hand point-
ing into the sea when we hailed the Long-boat a few
days after, gave me as heavy a shock and as sharp a
pang of heartache to bear as ever I remember suffering in
all my life. I only mention these things to show that if I

did give way a little at first, under the dread that our captain was lost to us, it was not without having been a good deal shaken beforehand by more trials of one sort or another than often fall to one man's share.

I had got over the choking in my throat with the help of a drop of water, and had steadied my mind again so as to be prepared against the worst, when I heard the hail (Lord help the poor fellows, how weak it sounded!), "Surf-boat, ahoy!"

I looked up, and there were our companions in misfortune tossing abreast of us not so near that we could make out the features of any of them, but near enough, with some exertion for people in our condition, to make their voices heard in the intervals when the wind was weakest.

I answered the hail, and waited a bit, and heard nothing, and then sung out the captain's name. The voice that replied did not sound like his; the words that reached us were:

"Chief mate wanted on board!"

Every man of my crew knew what that meant as well as I did. As second officer in command, there could be but one reason for wanting me on board the Long-boat. A groan went all round us, and my men looked darkly in each other's faces and whispered under their breaths:

"The captain is dead!"

I commanded them to be silent, and not to make too sure of bad news, at such a pass as things had now come to with us. Then, hailing the Long-boat, I signified that I was ready to go on board when the weather would let me—stopped a bit to draw a good long breath—

and then called out as loud as I could the dreadful question:

"Is the captain dead?"

The black figures of three or four men in the after-part of the Long-boat all stooped down together as my voice reached them. They were lost to view for about a minute, then appeared again. One man among them was held up on his feet by the rest, and he hailed back the blessed words (a very faint hope went a very long way with people in our desperate situation):

"Not yet!"

The relief felt by me, and by all with me, when we knew that our captain, though unfitted for duty, was not lost to us, it is not in words—at least, not in such words as a man like me can command—to express. I did my best to cheer the men by telling them what a good sign it was that we were not as badly off yet as we had feared; and then communicated what instructions I had to give to William Rames, who was to be left in command in my place when I took charge of the Long-boat. After that, there was nothing to be done but to wait for the chance of the wind dropping at sunset, and the sea going down afterwards, so as to enable our weak crews to lay the two boats alongside of each other without undue risk—or, to put it plainer, without saddling ourselves with the necessity for any extraordinary exertion of strength or skill. Both the one and the other had now been starved out of us for days and days together.

At sunset the wind suddenly dropped, but the sea, which had been running high for so long a time past, took hours after that before it showed any signs of getting to rest. The moon was shining, the sky was wonderfully clear, and it could not have been, according to my calculations, far off midnight when the long, slow, regular swell of the calming ocean fairly set in, and I took the responsibility of lessening the distance between the Long-boat and ourselves.

It was, I dare say, a delusion of mine; but I thought I had never seen the moon shine so white and ghastly anywhere, either at sea or on land, as she shone that night while we were approaching our companions in misery. When there was not much more than a boat's length between us, and the white light streamed cold and clear over all our faces, both crews rested on their oars with one great shudder, and stared over the gunwale of either boat, panic-stricken at the first sight of each other.

"Any lives lost among you?" I asked, in the midst of that frightful silence.

The men in the Long-boat huddled together like sheep at the sound of my voice.

"None yet, but the child, thanks be to God!" answered one among them.

And at the sound of his voice, all my men shrank together like the men in the Long-boat. I was afraid to let the horror produced by our first meeting at close quarters after the dreadful changes that wet, cold and famine had produced, last one moment longer than could be helped; so, without giving time for any more questions and answers, I commanded the men to lay the two boats close alongside of each other. When I rose up and committed the tiller to the hands of Rames, all my poor fellows raised their white faces imploringly to mine. "Don't leave us, sir," they said, "don't leave us." "I leave you," says I, "under the command and the guidance of Mr. William Rames, as good a sailor as I am, and as trusty and kind a man as ever stepped. Do your duty by him, as you have done it by me; and remember, to the last, that while there is life there is hope. God bless and help you all!" With those words, I collected what strength I had left, caught at two arms that were held out to me, and so got from the stern-sheets of one boat into the stern-sheets of the other.

"Mind where you step, sir," whispered one of the men who had helped me into the Long-boat. I looked down as he spoke. Three figures were huddled up below me, with the moonshine falling on them in ragged streaks through the gaps between the men standing or sitting above them. The first face I made out was the face of Miss Coleshaw; her eyes were wide open, and fixed on me. She seemed still to keep her senses and, by the alternate parting and closing of her lips, to be trying to speak, but I could not hear that she uttered a single word. On her shoulder rested the head of Mrs. Atherfield. The mother of our poor little Golden Lucy must, I think, have been dreaming of the child she had lost, for there was a faint smile just ruffling the white stillness of her face, when I first saw it turned upward, with peaceful closed eyes towards the heavens. From her, I looked down a little and there, with his head on her lap, and with one of her hands resting tenderly on his cheek—there lay the captain, to whose help and guidance, up to this miserable time, we had never looked in vain; there, worn out at last in our service, and for our sakes, lay the best and bravest man of all our company. I stole my hand in gently through his clothes and laid it on his heart, and felt a little feeble warmth over it, though my cold, dulled touch could not detect even the faintest beating. The two men in the stern-sheets with me, noticing what I was doing—knowing I loved him like a brother—and seeing, I suppose, more distress in my face than I myself was conscious of its showing, lost command over themselves altogether, and burst into a piteous moaning, sobbing lamentation over him. One of the two drew aside a jacket from his feet, and showed me that they were bare, except where a wet ragged strip of stocking still clung to one of them. When the ship struck the iceberg, he had to run on deck, leaving his shoes in his cabin. All through the voyage in the boat his feet had been unprotected; and not a soul had discovered it until he dropped! As long as he could keep his eyes open, the very look of them had cheered the men, and comforted and upheld the women. Not one living creature in the boat, with any sense about him, but had felt the good influence of that brave man in one way or another. Not one but had heard him, over and over again, give the credit to others which was due only to himself; praising this man for patience, and thanking that man for help, when the patience and the help had really and truly, as to the best part of both, come only from him. All this, and much more, I heard pouring confusedly from the men's lips while they crouched down, sobbing and crying over their commander, and wrapping the jacket as warmly and tenderly as they could over his cold feet. It went to my heart to check them; but I knew that if this lamenting spirit spread any further, all chance of keeping alight any last sparks of hope and resolution among the boat's company would be lost for ever. Accordingly, I sent them to their places, spoke a few encouraging words to the men forward, promising to serve out, when the morning came, as much as I dared of any eatable thing left in the lockers; called to Rames, in my old boat, to keep as near us as he safely could; drew the garments and coverings of the two poor suffering women more closely about them; and, with a secret prayer to be directed for the best in bearing the awful responsibility now laid on my shoulders, took my captain's vacant place at the helm of the Long-boat.

This, as well as I can tell it, is the full and true account of how I came to be placed in charge of the lost passengers and crew of the *Golden Mary*, on the morning of the twenty-seventh day after the ship struck the iceberg and foundered at sea.

Before I go on to relate what happened after the two boats were under my command, I will stop a little here, for the purpose of adding some pages of writing to the present narrative without which it would not be, in my humble estimation, complete. I allude to some little record of the means by which—before famine and suffering dulled our ears and silenced our tongues—we shortened the weary hours and helped each other to forget, for a while, the dangers that encompassed us. The stories to which Captain Ravender has referred as having been related by the people in his boat, were matched by other stories, related by the people in my boat; and in both cases, as I well know, the good effect of our following, in this matter, the example of Bligh and his men, when they were adrift like us, was of unspeakable importance in keeping up our spirits and, by consequence, in giving us the courage which was necessary, under Providence, to the preservation of our lives. I shall therefore ask permission, before proceeding to the account of our Deliverance, to reproduce in this place three or four of the most noteworthy of the stories which circulated among us. Some, I give from my remembrance; some, which I did not hear, from the remembrance of others.

PART TWO

"The Beguilement in the Boats"

CHAPTER I

I COME from Ashbroke. (It was the armourer who spun this yarn.) Dear me! How many years back is that? Twenty years ago it must be now, long before I ever thought of going to sea, before I let rambling notions get into my head—when I used to walk up the street singing, and thinking of the time when I should come to have a forge of my own.

It was a pretty sight to look down Ashbroke, especially on a fine summer's day, when the sun was out. Why, I've been told painters would come from miles off purposely to put it down on paper, and you'd see them at turnings of the road and under trees working away like bees. And no wonder; for I have seen pictures enough in my day, but none to go near that. I've often wished I could handle a brush like some of those people—just enough, you know, to make a little picture of it for myself, to bring about with me and hang up over my hammock. For that matter, I am looking at it this moment, standing, as it might be, at the corner of the road, looking down the slope. There was the old church, just here on the right, with a slanting roof running to the ground, almost. You might walk round it for a month and not see a bare stone, the moss grew so thick all over it. It was very pleasant of Sundays, standing by and seeing the village folk trooping out of the porch, and hearing the organ-music playing away inside! Then, going down the hill, a little further on, you met queer, old-fashioned houses, with great shingle roofs. Beyond that, again, was a puzzling bit of building, like the half of a church window, standing up quite stiff by itself. They used to say there had once been an abbey or nunnery in these parts, full of clergymen and clergywomen, in the old Papist times, of course; and there were little bits of it sticking up all over the place. Then more old houses (how the moss did grow, to be sure!) until you passed by the Joyful Heart Inn, where every traveller pulled up to refresh himself and his nag. Many is the pleasant hour I've spent in the Joyful Heart, sitting in the cool porch with the ivy hanging down overhead, or by the great fireplace in the sanded kitchen.

There was a sort of open place in front of the Joyful Heart, with a market-cross in the middle, and a spring where the young women used to come for water and stand talking there, telling each other the news. The painters used to put them down, too—spring and all; and I don't wonder their fancying them. For, when I was sitting that way in the porch, looking out at them, the red petticoats and the queer jars, and the old cross, and the sun going down behind made a kind of picture, very pretty to look at. I've seen the same of it many a time in some of those places about the Spanish Main, when the foreign women stood round about and carried their jars in the same fashion. Only there was no Joyful Heart. I always missed the Joyful Heart in such places. Neither was there the Great Forge just over the way, facing the Joyful Heart. I must put in a word here about the Forge, though I have been a long time coming round to the point.

I never saw such a forge as that—never! It must have been another bit of the old abbey—the great gate, most likely, for it was nothing but a huge, wide archway. Very handsomely worked, though, and covered with moss like the rest. There was a little stone hutch at the top that looked like a belfry. The bell was gone long ago, of course, but the rings were there and the stauncheons, all soundly made—good work as I could have turned out myself. Someone had run up a bit of building at the back, which kept out the wind and made all snug, and there you had as handsome a forge as I ever came across.

It was kept by a young man of the name of Whichelo —Will Whichelo. But he had another name besides that, and I think a better one. If you were to go asking through the village for one Will Whichelo, why, you would come back about as wise as you went; unless, indeed, you chanced upon the minister or the school-master. No; but because he was always seen hard at his work, swinging his hammer with good-will, and stepping back at every stroke to get a better sweep—because he laid his whole soul into the business—the Ashbroke folk christened him Ding Dong Will. He was always singing and at his work. Many a nice young woman of the village would have been glad if Ding Dong Will had looked her way. But he never took heed of any of them, or was more than civil and gentle with them.

"Look ye," he would say, leaning on his great hammer, "are they the creatures for handling cold iron, or lifting the sledge? No, no!" and would take up his favourite stave of Hammer and anvil! hammer and anvil! lads, yoho!

I was but a youngster at that time, but had a great hankering after the iron business. I would be nothing else, I told my father, who wanted to send me up to London to learn accounts. I was always dropping down there, and would stay half the day, leaning against the arch and watching the forging. Coming along of a night, I used to get quite cheerful when I saw the blaze of the furnace, and the chinking of the iron was the finest music for me I ever heard—finer than the organ tunes even. Sometimes a dusty rider would come galloping in, and pull up sharp at the Forge; he had cast a shoe on the road, and Ding Dong Will would come out and take the horse's measure. Then the village folk would get standing round, in twos and threes, all of them eyeing over the horse and rider, too. Then he would get upon his nag once more, and the little crowd would open, and he ride away harder than he came, Ding Dong Will, with his hammer over his shoulder, looking after him till he got to the turn of the hill.

At last, my father came round and gave up making me a clerk—it would never have done—and Ding Dong Will, who had a liking for me, agreed to take me at the Forge. I soon got to use the big sledge fairly enough —nothing, of course, to Ding Dong Will; and so we worked away from morning till night, like two Jolly Millers. There was fine music at the Forge, when the two of us were at it.

Ding Dong Will never went to the Joyful Heart, he said he had no time to be idle; but I went pretty often—that is, when the day was done and work over —just to have a talk in the cool porch and hear what company was in the house. For Miss Arthur—Mary Arthur, she that used to sit in the parlour and manage the house, was never very stand-off to me. But she had a reason of her own for that, as you will see. She was niece to old Joe Fenton, the landlord, who brought her down from London to keep things going. In short, she was as good as mistress there. Folks said she kept her head a little high; but, to say truth, I never found her so. She had had her schooling up in London, and had learned manners with the best of them, so it was but nature she should be a stroke above the girls of the place. That was why they didn't like her. About her looks? Ah! she was a beauty! Such hair—it went nigh down to her feet; and her eyes, why they shot fire like a pair of stars; and she had a way of shifting them back and forward, and taking your measure at every look, that made you feel quite uneasy. All the young fellows were by the ears about her, but she never heeded or encouraged them; unless it might be that she had a leaning to one—and that was to Ding Dong Will opposite. No one thought of such a thing, she kept it so close; but she might as well have had a leaning to a lump of cold iron.

The way I came to suspect it was this. The old Forge, as I said, was just fronting the Joyful Heart; and every morning, as sure as I came down to work, I used to see her sitting in the bow-window, behind the white curtain, working with her needle. There she would be all the morning, for at that time there was nothing doing downstairs, and, every now and again, she would be taking a sly look over at the Forge where Ding Dong Will was swinging his great sledge, and trolling his Hammer and anvil! lads, yoho! He was well worth looking out at, was Ding Dong Will. I used to tell him, "Mary Arthur is making eyes at you yonder—have a care, Will." And he would laugh loud, and say, "She may find better sport elsewhere. No sweethearts for me, lad. Hand the file. Sing Hammer and anvil, yoho!"

I never saw so insensible a fellow, never. But her liking slipped out in more ways than that. Whenever I went in, she was always taking notice of me, and asking about myself. How was I getting on at the Forge? Did I like the business? Did we do much? What kind was he, the other—he with the curious name? Then she would laugh, and show her white teeth.

At last, one Saturday evening I was sitting in the porch, looking at the children playing in the road, when I heard a step at the back, and there was Mary Arthur standing behind me. "Resting after the week?" she said.

"Yes, and a hard week we've had of it."

"Nothing doing at the Forge now, I suppose," says she. (He had gone down to the green with the young fellows to throw the bar.)

"No," says I; "we've let the fire out, and will rest till Monday."

She stayed silent for a minute, and then: "Why does he—Whichelo I mean—keep shut up that way at home?" She was beating her hands impatiently together. "What does it all mean? What do you make of it?"

I stared, you may be sure, she spoke so sharply.

"Does he never go out and see the world—go to dances or merry-makings?"

"No," said I, "never."

"Well," said she, "isn't it odd; how do you account for it?"

"Well, it is odd," I said.

"And he's so young!"

All this while she was shifting her black eyes in a restless kind of way.

"You should try," says she, "and get him to mix more with the others, for your own sake as well as his."

I was going to tell her I was at him morning, noon and night, when the bell rang, and she tripped off.

Ding Dong Will came into the Forge that night fairly

73

tired and done up. "Beat them as usual!" he said, as he flung himself down on the bench.

"I knew you would," I said.

"But it was thirsty work; some drink, for Heaven's sake!"

"There's not a drop of malt in the house," I said.

"Well, go over and fetch some."

Said I: "Go yourself. I tell you what, there's a nice girl there always talking of you; and, if you've anything of a man about you, you'll go over and speak to her softly, and show her you're not what she takes you for. Now, there's my mind for you, Ding Dong Will."

"Stuff," says he, laughing; "let her mind her own business, and leave me to my anvil. I'll not go."

"Ah! you're afraid," said I, "that's it!"

"Afraid," says he, starting up, "you know I'm not— you know I'm not. Here, I'll go," and made straight for the door. "Stop," he said, turning round, "what did she say about taking me for a different sort of man?"

"No matter now," said I. "When you come back".

It should have been a five minutes' job, that fetching the malt. But, would you believe it? He was close upon an hour about it. I knew well she had not been losing her time. When he came in, I began at once at him: "Ah, ah!" said I, "didn't I tell you? I knew it!"

"Nonsense," said he, with a foolish kind of laugh, "it was none of my fault. She kept me there with her talk, and I couldn't get away."

"O, poor Ding Dong Will," I said, "you had better have stayed away, after all!"

"Folly!" says he, laughing more foolishly still, "you'll

see if she gets me there again. Enough about her. There!"

I saw he was uneasy in his mind, and so gave him no more trouble. But I needn't have been so delicate with him at all, for next day it was quite the other way. He never gave me peace or rest, sounding me and picking out of me what she had said of him. The man was clean gone from that hour. It's always the way with those kind of men—when they are touched, they run off like a bit of melted metal.

He got worse every day from that out. He was in and out of the Joyful Heart half his time, always on some excuse or other, and going lazily to his work, stopping every now and again to have a look at the white curtain over the way. It was a poor thing to see him— it was indeed; I was ashamed of him. At last he came to doing nothing at all, or next to nothing, and the great hammer was laid by in a corner.

Well, this went on it might be for a month, and folks in the village began to talk and wink, and say, what would come next, now that Ding Dong Will was caught at last. I tried to keep things going as well as I could, but it was of very little use. The business fell off; and I will never forget the sinking feeling I got when the riders began to go straight on through the village—past the old Forge—and pull up at a new place, lately opened, beyond the church! After all, they only did what was natural, and went where they would be best attended to. By-and-by I saw a change coming on Ding Dong Will —a very odd change. With all his foolishness, he had been in great spirits—always laughing—without much meaning to be sure; but, still as I say, in great spirits. But now I saw that he was turning quite another way, getting quite a down-hearted, moping kind of manner I couldn't well make out. He would come in of an evening—very rough and sulky—and sit down before the fire looking into the coals, and never open his mouth for hours at a time. Then he would get up and walk up and down, stamping and muttering—nothing very holy, you may be sure. I soon guessed—indeed, I heard as much in the village—that she was drawing off a bit, or else trying her play-acting upon him, for she was full of those kind of tricks. She was a very deep one, that Mary Arthur, and it was a pity she ever came into the place. She had a kind of up-and-down way of treating him, one time being all smiles and pleasantness, and next day like a lump of ice, pretending not to see him when he came in. She made him know his place, rolling her black eyes back and forward in every direction but his; then he would come home raging and swearing. I often wondered what she could be at, or what was at the bottom of it all; and, I believe I would never have come to the truth if I didn't happen one day to run up against a handsome-looking gentleman in a fisherman's hat, just at the door of the Joyful Heart. They told me, inside, it was young Mr. Temple, of Temple Court—some ten miles off—come down to stop there for the fishing.

There it was! That was the secret of all! He had been there nigh on a fortnight—had come, mind you, for two or three days' fishing; but the sport was so good he really must stay a bit longer. Quite natural and, you may say, quite proper! I'm thinking there was better sport going on in the parlour than ever he found in the river. Her head was nigh turned with it all, and I really believe she thought she was going to be mistress of Temple Court before long, though how a young girl that had come down to London, and had seen a bit of life, should be so short-seeing, is more than I can fancy. She took the notion into her head, that was certain, and every soul in the place could see what she was at, except the poor blind creature at the Forge; but even he had his eyes opened at last, for people now began to talk and whisper, and hope all was right up at the Joyful Heart. I heard that the minister had gone once to speak with her, but came out very red and angry. No doubt she had bidden him mind his own concerns, and not meddle with her. As to old Joe Fenton's looking after his niece, he might as well have been cut out of a block of wood.

One morning, just after breakfast, when he—Ding Dong Will—was sitting at the fire as usual, and not speaking a word, he turns round quite sharp upon me and says:

"What is that young Jack doing all this time? What do you say?"

"I'm sure I can't tell," I said, "unless it be fishing."

"Fishing!" said he, stamping down the coals with his great shoe, "like enough! I've never heard much of the fish in these waters."

"Still, he does go out with a rod," I said, "there's nothing else here to amuse him, I suppose. But he goes on Monday."

"Look me in the face," says he, catching me by the wrist, "you don't believe that he's come only for that?"

"I can't tell," said I, "unless it is that he likes Mary Arthur's company. She's a nice girl!"

"Ah!" said he, "I've been thinking so some time back—the false, hollow jade! This was at the bottom of all her tricks! But I tell you what," said he, snatching his hammer, "let him look out, and not come in my way—I give him warning——."

With this he got a bit of iron upon the anvil and beat away at it like a wild man. Then he flung it down into a corner and, taking his hat, walked out with great strides. I ran after him and took him by the arm, for I was in a desperate fright lest he should do something wicked. But he put me back quietly.

"See," said he, "I give you a caution, don't meddle with me. Mind——."

I didn't try and stop him then, for he looked savage. But I followed a little behind. He made for the Joyful Heart; and, just as he came under the porch, with his head down, and never heeding where he was going to, he ran full up against somebody who, without much more ado, gave him back his own, and flung him right against the wall.

"Now then, young Hercules!" said a gay kind of voice—I knew it for Mr. Temple's—"now then, look before you, will you! Keep the passage clear."

I thought the other was going to run at him straight, but he stopped himself quickly.

"Who are you speaking to in that way?" said he, with

a low kind of growl. "Is it your horse, or your dog, or your groom? Which? Are those manners?"

"Now, Bruin," says the young man, "no words. Let me pass, I'm in a hurry."

"Who was it taught you," says Ding Dong Will, with the same kind of growl and not moving an inch, "who taught you to call folk Bruins and Herculeses—eh? I declare," says he, colouring up quite red, and trembling all over, "I've a mind to give you a lesson myself. I will, by——."

I think he was going to spring at him this time, but I heard steps on the sanded floor, and there was Mary Arthur standing before us. A fine creature she looked, too. She was in a tearing rage, and her eyes had more of the devilish look in them than I had ever seen before.

"For shame," she said, to Will, "for shame! What do you come here for, with your low brawling ways. Who asks you to come? Who wants you? Take him away—home, anywhere out of this!"

It was a piteous sight to look at poor Ding Dong Will, staring stupidly at her and breathing hard, as if there was a weight on his chest.

"Mr. Temple," says she, turning to him quite changed, and with a gentle smile on her face, "can you forgive me for all this? That such a thing should have happened to you in our house! But it shall never occur again! Never, never!"

I could see he took her very easy, for he was looking out at something, and she had to say it twice over before he heard her.

"Sweet Mary," said he, "don't give yourself a

moment's uneasiness about me. Let things go as they like, so that you don't put yourself out." Here he gave a kind of yawn, and went over to the window.

She looked after him biting her lip hard.

"Why don't you take him away, as I told you?" she says at last. "What does he want here?"

I pitied him so much, to see him standing there so beaten down, that I could not help putting in my word.

"Well, I must say, Miss Mary, poor Ding Dong Will didn't deserve this—from you, of all people."

"Hallo!" says Mr. Temple, coming back, "is this famous Ding Dong Will from over the way?"

"No other, sir," says I.

"Here, Ding Dong Will," says he, putting out his hand, "we mustn't fall out. If I had known it was you, you should have had the passage all to yourself. You're a fine fellow, Will, and I've often admired the way you swung the great hammer."

She was biting her lips still harder than before, but said nothing.

"Stop," said he, "I have a great idea. So this is Ding Dong Will! Whisper a minute, Mary."

He did whisper something to her, and you never saw what a change it made in her. She turned all scarlet, and gave him such a wicked, devilish look.

"This is some joke," said she, at last.

"Not a bit of it," says he, laughing, "not a bit of it. Ah! You see, I know what goes on in the village!"

"I couldn't believe that you mean such a thing!" says she, getting white again.

"Stuff!" said he, very impatiently. "I tell you, I am

in earnest. Listen, Ding Dong Will. I must be off to London to-morrow—the ladies there are dying to see me, so go I must. Now, I know there has been something on between you two—don't tell me. I know all about it. So now, friend Ding Dong, show yourself a man of spirit, and settle it sharp. And I promise you, I'll come down myself to give the bride away, and start you both comfortably."

It was well for him he was looking the other way, and didn't see the infernal look she gave him out of those eyes of hers. I think if there had been a knife convenient, she would have plunged it into him at that minute. But she covered it all with a kind of forced laugh, and said she wasn't quite ready to be disposed of so quickly, and then made some excuse to run upstairs. Mr. Temple then yawned again and went over to the window, and wondered would it be a fine night, as he had to dine out. Neither of us spoke to him, for he was an unfeeling fellow with all his generous offers. So we left him there, and I brought back Ding Dong Will to the Forge again.

About four o'clock that same day (it was almost dark at that hour), when I was coming home from buying something in the village, I thought I saw him crossing over to the Joyful Heart, and as I passed the porch, I swear I saw the two of them (Mary Arthur and he) talking in the passage—there was no mistake about it, and she talking very eagerly. Presently she drew him into the parlour, and shut the door. What could bring him there now, after the morning's business? Well, I thought, he is a poor-spirited creature, after all—

a true spaniel! He didn't come in, I suppose, for an hour after that, and then in a wild sort of humour, as if he had been drinking. But what do you think of his denying that he had been near the Joyful Heart at all, or that he had seen her? Denied it flat! And then, when I pressed him on it, and asked if I wasn't to trust my own eyes, he began to show his teeth and get savage. I was only a youngster then, and so had to put up with his humours; but I determined to leave him on the first convenient excuse. Dear! How that man was changed in a short time!

On this night he took a fancy that we should go to bed early. He was tired, he said, and wanted rest after the day's trouble, and his heart was heavy. So I gave in to him at once, and we were soon snug in our little cots on each side of the hearth; we used to sleep of nights in a queer kind of place just off the forge, all vaulted over, with arches crossing one another and meeting in a kind of carved bunch in the middle. This might have been the clergymen's pantry, or wine vaults, maybe, in the old times. Whatever use they had for it, it was a very snug place. I recollect there were all sorts of queer faces with horns and hoods, all carved out in the bunch; and I often lay awake at nights looking at them and studying them, and thinking why they were grinning and winking at me in that way. I remember one creature that always aimed straight at you with his tail pointed, holding it like a gun.

It must have been about nine o'clock, or perhaps half-past eight, when we turned in. I know I heard the old church clock chiming pleasantly as we lay down. After watching the fire flashing up and down, and taking a look at the funny faces in the bunch overhead, I soon went sound asleep. I woke again, before the fire was out, and looking towards Will's cot saw that it was empty. A vague feeling of uneasiness mingled with my surprise at that discovery, and made me jump out of bed in a moment. I reflected for a little, felt more uneasy than ever, huddled on my clothes in a great hurry and, without giving myself a moment's time for any second thoughts, went out to see what had become of Ding Dong Will.

He was not in the neighbourhood of the Forge, so I followed a steep footpath in the wood behind which led straight to the water's edge. I walked on a little, observing that the moon was out and the stars shining, and the sky of a fine frosty blue, until I came to an old tree that I knew well. I had hardly cast a first careless look at it, before I started back all in a fright, for I saw at my feet, stretched out among the leaves, a figure with a fisherman's hat beside it. I knew it to be young Mr. Temple, lying there quite dead, with his face all over blood. I thought I should have sunk down upon the earth with grief and horror, and ran farther along the little pathway as far as I could to a place where the trees opened a little, full in the moonlight. There I saw Ding Dong Will standing quite still and motionless, with his hammer on his shoulder and his face covered up in his hand.

He stayed a long time that way, without ever stirring, and then began to come up very slowly, weeping, his eyes upon the ground. I felt as if I were fixed to that one spot, and waited till he met me full face to face. What a guilty start he gave! I thought he would have dropped.

"O, Will, Will! What have you been doing? Some terrible thing!"

"I—I—I, nothing!" he said, staggering about, and hiding his face.

"What have you done with him—Mr. Temple?" I said, still holding him. He was trembling all over like a palsied man, and fell back against a tree with a deep groan. I saw how it was then—it was as good as written in his face. So I left him there against the tree, and all the rest of that horrible night I wandered up and down along the roads and lanes; anything sooner than be under the same roof with him. At last morning came and, as soon as the sun rose I stole back and, looking through the window, found that he was gone. I never like to think of that night, though it is so far back.

By noon the next day the whole town was in a fever; people talking and whispering at corners. He had been missed; but they were on his track, for it was well known that he was away among the hills hiding. They dragged the river all day and, on that night, the body of young Mr. Temple was found, his head beaten in with a hammer.

What end Will Whichelo came to it would not be hard to guess. But Mary Arthur, she who drove him on to it, as everybody knew—she was let away, and went up to London, where she lived to do mischief enough. The old Forge was shut up, and fell into greater ruin. For many a long day no one ventured near that part of the river walk after dark.

CHAPTER II

IT was the fifth evening, towards twilight, when poor
Dick began to sing—in my boat, the Surf-boat.
At first nobody took any notice of him and, indeed,
he seemed to be singing more to himself than to anyone else. I had never heard the tune before, neither
have I heard it since, but it was beautiful. I don't know
how it might sound now, but then, in the twilight,
darkness coming down on us fast and, for aught we
knew, death in the darkness, its simple words were full
of meaning. The song was of a mother and child talking
together of Heaven. I saw more than one gaunt face

lifted up, and there was a great sob when it was done, as if everybody had held their breath to listen. Says Dick then, "That was my cousin Amy's song, Mr. Steadiman."

"Then it will be a favourite of yours, Dick," I replied, hazarding a guess at the state of the case.

"Yes. I don't know why I sing it. Perhaps she put it in my mind. Do you believe in those things, Mr. Steadiman?"

"In what things, Dick?" I wanted to draw him on to talk of himself, as he had no other story to tell.

"She's dead, captain, and it seemed a little while since as if I heard her voice, far away, as it might be in England, singing it again; and when she stopped, I took it up. It must be fancy, you know, it could not really be." Before long the night fell, and when we could not see each other's faces—except by the faint starlight—it seemed as if poor Dick's heart opened, and as if must tell us who and what he was.

Perhaps I ought to say how poor Dick came to be with us at all. About a week before we sailed, there came to Captain Ravender one morning at his inn a man whom he had known intimately, when they two were young fellows. Said he, "Captain, there's my nephew—poor Dick Tarrant. I want to ship him off to Australia, to California, or anywhere out of the way. He does nothing but get into mischief here and bring disgrace on the family. Where are you bound for, next voyage?" Captain Ravender replied, "California." "California is a long way off," said Captain Ravender's friend, "it will do as well as any place;

he can dig for gold. The fact is, Dick has run through one fortune, and now a maiden-aunt, who considers the credit of the family, offers him three hundred pounds to leave England. He consents to go, and the best plan will be to put him under your charge, pay his passage and outfit, and leave the rest of the money in your hands to be given over to him when he lands at the diggings."

Captain Ravender agreed to the proposal, and poor Dick, who had been left standing outside the door, was called in and introduced. I came in just at that point, and saw him. He was the wreck of what had been a fine-looking young man ten years ago, dragged down now by reckless dissipation to reckless poverty. His clothing was very shabby, his countenance wild and haggard, his shock of brown hair rusty with neglect —not a promising subject to look at. His uncle told him the arrangements he had made with Captain Ravender, in which he apparently acquiesced without much caring. "North or south, east or west," said he, "it was all the same to him. If he had gone out to India, when he had a chance a dozen years before, he should have been a man or a mouse then." That was the only remark he offered. And the thing was settled.

But when the time came to sail, poor Dick was not forthcoming. We sent up to his uncle's house to know what was to be done, and, by-the-by, down he came with his nephew, who had almost given us the slip. Until we got into blue water Dick was prisoner rather than passenger. He did not take to his punishment kindly, or see, as his relatives did, that there was a chance before him of redeeming a wasted life and repairing a ruined constitution. He was a very good-humoured, easy-tempered fellow, and a great favourite aboard, and, till the time of the wreck, cheerful, except in the evening when he got to leaning over the ship's side, and singing all kinds of sentimental love-songs. I had told the men to keep an eye on him, and they did. I was afraid he might, in one of his black moods, try to make away with himself.

He was the younger of two brothers, sons of a yeoman or gentleman farmer in Cheshire, both whose parents died when they were quite little things, leaving them, however, for their station, amply provided for. There was two hundred pounds a year for their bringing-up, till they were eighteen, when the sum was to be doubled, and at one-and-twenty they were to get five thousand pounds a-piece to start them in the world. Old Miss Julian Tarrant took Tom, the elder, and my friend took poor Dick. Dick was a wild lad, idle at his book, hankering after play, but as kind-hearted and handsome a fellow as you could wish to see. Dick was generally better liked than Tom, who was steady as old Time. Both brothers were sent to the grammar school of the town, near which they lived, and one of Dick's discursive anecdotes related to the second master there whom, he asserted, he should have had pleasure in soundly thrashing at that moment, in part payment of the severe punishment he had formerly inflicted on his idle pupil. When Dick was sixteen that tide in his affairs came which, had he followed it out to India, would probably have led on to fortune. But Dick had an invincible tie to England. Precocious in every-thing, he was deeply in love with his cousin Amy, who was three years older than himself, and very beautiful; and Amy was very fond of him as of a younger brother.

Said poor Dick, with a quiver in his voice, as he was telling his story, "She was the only creature in the whole world that ever really cared whether I lived or died. I worshipped the very ground she walked on! Tom was a clever, shrewd fellow—made for getting on in the world, and never minding anybody but him-self. Uncle Tarrant was as hard and rigid as a machine, and his wife was worse—there was nobody nice but Amy; she was an angel! When I got into scrapes, and spent more money than I ought, she set me right with my uncle, and later—when it was too late for any good, and the rest of them treated me like a dog—she never gave me either a cold look or a hard word. Bless her!"

For the sake of being near his cousin, Dick professed a wish to be a farmer like his cousin and father, which was quite agreeable to the family, and for three years more he stayed in his Uncle Tarrant's house, very much beloved by all—though in his bitterness he said not—for his gaiety and light heart were like a charm about him. If there was a fault, he had friends too many, for most of them were of a kind not likely to profit a young man.

Coming home one evening, about twilight, from a hunt which he had attended, the poor lad unexpectedly met the crisis of his fate. He told us this with an exactness of detail that made the scene he described like a bit of Dutch painting. I wish I could repeat it to you in his own words, but that is impossible; still, I will be as exact as possible.

In Mr. Tarrant's house there was a little parlour especially appropriated to Amy's use. It had a low window with a cushioned seat, from which one long step took you into the garden. In this parlour Amy had her piano, her book-case, her work-basket, her mother's picture on the wall, and several of poor Dick's sketches neatly framed. Dick liked this room better than any other in the house. When the difference betwixt Amy's age and his seemed greater than it did now, it was here he used to come to be helped with his lessons; and later, when his red-hot youth was secretly wreathing all manner of tender fancies about her, that he used to sit at her feet reading to her out of some poetry-book, or singing while she worked, or, perhaps, sang, too. These pleasant early intimacies had never been discontinued, for, while Dick's heart was wasting its first passion on his cousin, she was all the while thinking of somebody else. He was a boy to her in point of age still, and this particular day ended his blissful delusions.

Having put his pony in the stable, he made his way at once to Amy's parlour, opening the door softly, for he liked to surprise her. Neither she not the person with her heard him enter; they were too much occupied with themselves and each other to hear anything. Amy was standing in the window, and beside her, with his arm round her waist, was the straight-haired, pale-featured curate of the parish. It was a clear yellow twilight, and all about Amy's head the lustre shone like a glory; her hands were down-dropped, and the busy fingers were plucking a rose to pieces, petal by petal, and scattering them on the carpet at her feet. She was as blushing herself as the poor rose, and seemed to listen willingly to the pleadings of her lover. Dick noticed the slight quivering of her lips and the humid glitter of her eyes when the low-spoken, tremulous words, meant only for one ear, met his, and he said he felt as if all the blood in his body were driven violently up to his brain by their sound.

The bird in its cage began trilling a loud song as it pecked at a spray of green which the evening wind blew against the wires through the open window, and under cover of its noise poor Dick stole out, leaving the young lovers alone in the blush of their acknowledged love. He went back to the stable, got his pony out, mounted it, and galloped away like mad to rejoin the companions he had left an hour before for Amy's sake. It was not till after midnight that he came home, and then he was reeling drunk. His Uncle Tarrant and Amy had sat up for him and, being quarrelsome in his cups, he insulted the first, and would not speak to his cousin. Poor Dick thought to drown his sorrow, and this was the beginning of his downward course.

The individual whom Amy had chosen to endow with her love had nothing about him particular to approve except his profession. All his attributes, moral, mental and personal, were negative rather than positive. Poor Dick described him only as straight-haired, as if that epithet embodied all his qualities. He thought that Amy did not really love him, but was attracted by some imaginary sanctity and perfection with which her imagination invested him. It was very likely; from what we see every day we may be sure that many women have loved not the man himself they have married, but an ideal which he personates very indifferently indeed to all eyes but theirs.

Dick could not, for many days, restrain the expression of his feelings. Coming one day suddenly on Amy in the garden where she was walking in maiden meditation, he stopped her and made her listen to his story, which he poured out with much exaggeration of epithet and manner. Amy was startled and distressed; she endeavoured in vain to stop his confession by appealing to his common sense of what was right.

"Dick, you know I am engaged to Henry Lister; you ought not to have spoken—let me go!" said she, for he had grasped her hands tightly in his.

"I ought not to have spoken, and I love! O! cousin, you don't know what love is if you say so. Amy, it will out! Amy, if I had come before the straight-haired parson, would you have listened to me then?"

A vivid blush flew into the girl's face, but she would not say a word of encouragement; on that blush, however, poor Dick, whether rightly or wrongly, contrived to found a renewed hope. Amy kept his avowal to herself, knowing well that its discovery would entail a total separation from her cousin; and she had become so accustomed to his usefulness and gaiety in a house where everybody else was chilly and methodical, that she could not readily part with him. I incline to think myself that she did like Dick better than the straight-haired curate for many reasons, and Dick himself was persuaded of it. Her indecision had, as may be supposed, a very pernicious effect on his mind and conduct. One day he was in the seventh heaven of hope and content-ment, and the next he was the most miserable dog alive; then he would go and forget his griefs in a convivial bout with his comrades, till at length his Uncle Tarrant turned him out of doors. Amy had tried her influence with him in vain.

"You are the cause of it, Amy, and nobody but you," said Dick, passionately. "If you would give that straight-haired fellow warning, you should never have to complain of me again."

But Amy, though she fretted a great deal, held to her engagement, and Dick went on from bad to worse.

It must have been very deplorable to behold the reckless way in which he dissipated his money as soon as he got it into his hands, ruining at once his prospects, his character and his health. With a temperament that naturally inclined him to self-indulgence, the road to ruin was equally rapid and pleasant. When Amy married Henry Lister—which she did after an engagement of six months—Dick kept no bounds, and he irretrievably offended his family by intruding himself, uninvited, amongst the guests at the wedding. There was a painful scene in Amy's parlour, where he went secretly, as he himself acknowledged, in the wild hope of inducing her to break off the engagement at the eleventh hour. She was dressed ready for church, and her mother was with her. That made no difference. Poor Dick went down on his knees, and cried, and kissed his cousin's hands, and besought her to listen to him. And Amy fainted. She fainted a second time at the altar when Dick forced himself into her presence and forbade the marriage. He was so frantic, so out of himself, that he had to be removed by compulsory measures before the service could go on. Of course, after a scene like this, his uncle's family kept no terms with him; he was forbidden ever to suffer his shadow to darken their door again—and so the poor, wild, crazed fellow went headlong to destruction. I doubt very much myself whether Amy was worth such a sacrifice; but he thought so. Life, he said, was unendurable without her, and he did not care how soon he ended it.

But this was not all. Amy died of consumption within a year of her marriage, and Dick asserted that she had been killed by bad usage. He went down to his uncle's house where she lay, and asked to see her. The request was refused, and he forced his way by the window into the room by night, as was afterwards discovered by the disarrangement of the furniture, and stayed there crying over his dead love until dawn. At her funeral he joined the mourners, and showed more grief than any of them; but as the husband was turning away, he walked up to him, and shook his clenched fist in his face, crying:

"You killed her, you straight-haired dog!"

It was supposed that if he had not been restrained by the bystanders, he might have done him a mischief. His family gave it out that he was mad. Perhaps he was.

94

Dice, drinking and horse-racing now soon made an end of poor Dick's five thousand pounds. He lost every shred of self-respect, and herded with the lowest of the low. There is no telling how a man's troubles may turn him, love disappointments especially; poor Dick's turned him into a thorough scamp. He was a disgrace to the family and a misery to himself, but there was this good left in him amidst his degrading excesses—the capability of regretting. He never enjoyed his vices or ceased to feel the horrible debasement of them. He was seen at races, prize-fights and fairs, in rags and tatters; he was known to have wanted bread; he was suspected of theft and poaching; and his brother Tom rescued him once out of the streets, where he was singing songs disguised as a lame soldier. Tom allowed him a guinea a week, but before he had been in receipt of it a month he made the annuity over to an acquaintance for ten pounds, to take him to Doncaster, and this friend always went with him to receive the money, lest he should lose it, so that Dick suffered extremities while he was supposed to be at least fed and clothed by his family. Ten years of reckless debauchery and poignant misery reduced him to the state in which his Uncle Tarrant brought him to me; his Aunt Julia, who had brought Tom up, offered to give him money if he would go out of the country and never come back again. How he went out of it, I have told already.

When he ceased speaking, I said, to encourage him:

"You'll do well yet, Dick, if you keep steady, and we make land or are picked up."

"What can it be," said Dick, without particularly answering, "that brings all these old things over my mind? There's a child's hymn I and Tom used to say at my mother's knee when we were little ones keeps running through my thoughts. It's the stars, maybe; there was a little window by my bed that I used to watch them at—a window in my room at home in Cheshire—and if I was ever afraid, as boys will be after reading a good ghost story, I would keep on saying it till I fell asleep."

"That was a good mother of yours, Dick; could you say that hymn now, do you think? Some of us might like to hear it."

"It's as clear in my mind at this minute as if my mother was here listening to me," said Dick, and he repeated:

> "Hear my prayer, O! Heavenly Father,
>   Ere I lay me down to sleep;
> Bid Thy Angels, pure and holy,
>   Round my bed their vigil keep.

> "My sins are heavy, but Thy mercy
>   Far outweighs them every one;
> Down before Thy Cross I cast them,
>   Trusting in Thy help alone.

> "Keep me through this night of peril
>   Underneath its boundless shade;
> Take me to Thy rest, I pray Thee,
>   When my pilgrimage is made.

96

"None shall measure out Thy patience
    By the span of human thought;
None shall bound the tender mercies
    Which Thy Holy Son has bought.

"Pardon all my past transgressions,
    Give me strength for days to come;
Guide and guard me with Thy blessing
    Till Thy Angels bid me home."

After a while Dick drew his coat up over his head and lay down to sleep.

"Well, poor Dick!" thought I, "it is surely a blessed thing for you that—

"None shall measure out God's patience,
    By the span of human thought;
None shall bound the tender mercies
    Which His Holy Son has bought."

CHAPTER III

A QUIET and middle-aged gentleman passenger,
who was going to establish a Store out there
and had been a kind of supercargo aboard of us,
besides, told what follows.

She lay off Naarden—the good ship *Brocken Spectre*,
I mean—far out in the roads; and I often thought, as
I looked at her through the haze, what an ancient, ill-
favoured hulk it was. I suppose I came down some
three or four times that day, being in a lounging un-

satisfied state of mind, and took delight in watching the high, old-fashioned poop, as it rocked all day long in that one spot. I likened it to a French roof of the olden time, it was garnished with so many little windows; and over all was the great lantern, which might have served conveniently for the vane or cupola seen upon such structures. For all that, it was not unpicturesque, and would have filled a corner in a Vandervelde picture harmoniously enough. She was to sail at three o'clock next morning, and I was to be the solitary cabin passenger.

As evening came on, it grew prematurely dark and cloudy, while the waves acquired that dull indigo tint so significant of ugly weather. Raw gusts came sweeping in towards the shore, searching me through and through. I must own to a sinking of the heart as I took note of these symptoms, for a leaning towards ocean in any of its moods had never been one of my failings, and it augured but poorly for the state of the elements next morning. "It will have spent itself during the night," I muttered, doubtfully, and turned back to the inn to eat dinner with what comfort I might.

The place of entertainment stood by itself upon a bleak sandy hill. From its window I could see, afar off, three lights rising and falling together, just where the high poop and lantern had been performing the same ocean-dance in the daytime. I was sitting by the fire, listening ruefully to the wind, when news was brought to me that the captain, Van Steen, had come ashore, and was waiting below to see me.

I found him walking up and down outside—a short, thick-set man, as it were, built upon the lines of his own vessel.

99

"Well, captain, you wished to see me," I said.

"Look to this, my master," he said, bluntly. "There's a gale brewing yonder, and wild weather coming. So just see to this. If we're not round the Helder Head by to-morrow night, we may have to beat round the bay for days and days. So look to it, master, and come aboard while there is time."

"I'm ready at any moment," I said, "but how do you expect to get round now? The sea is high enough as it is."

"No matter; the wind may be with us in the morning. We must clear the Head before to-morrow night. Why, look you," he added, sinking his voice, mysteriously, "I wouldn't be off Helder to-morrow night—no, not for a sack of guilders!"

"What do you mean?"

"Why, don't you know? It's Christmas night. Jan Fangel's night—Captain Jan's!"

"Well?"

"He comes to Helder to-morrow night; he is seen in the Bay. But we are losing time, master," said he, seizing my arm. "Get your things ready; these lads will carry them to the boat."

Three figures here advanced out of the shadow, and entered with me. I hastily paid the bill, and set forward with the captain for the shore, where the boat was waiting. My mails were got on board with all expedition, and we were soon far out upon the waters, making steadily for the three lights. It was not blowing very hard as yet, neither had the waves assumed the shape of what are known as white horses; but there was a heavy underground swell, and a peculiar swooping motion quite as disagreeable. Suddenly, I made out the great lantern just overhead, shining dimly, as it were through a fog. We had glided under the shadow of a dark mass, wherein there were many more dim lights at long intervals—and all together seemed performing a wild dance to the music of dismal creaking of timbers and rattling of chains. As we came under, a voice hailed us out of the darkness—as it seemed, from the region of the lantern; and presently invisible hands cast us ropes, whereby, with infinite pains and labour, I was got on deck. I was then guided down steep ways into the cabin, the best place for me under the circumstances. As soon as the wind changed, the captain said, we would put out to sea.

By the light of a dull oil-lamp overhead, that never for a moment ceased swinging, I tried to make out what my new abode was like. It was of an ancient massive fashion, with a dark oak panelling all round, rubbed smooth in many places by wear of time and friction. All round were queer little nobs and projections, mounted in brass and silver, just like the butt-ends of pistols; while here and there were snug recesses that reminded me of canons' stalls in a cathedral. The swinging lamp gave but a faint yellow light, that scarcely reached beyond the centre of the room, so that the oak-work all round cast little grotesque shadows, which had a very gloomy and depressing effect. There was a sort of oaken shelf at one end—handsomely wrought, no doubt, but a failure as to sleeping capabilities. Into this I introduced myself without delay, and soon fell off into a profound slumber, for I was weary enough.

When I awoke again, I found there was a figure standing over me who said he was Mr. Bode, the mate, who wished to know, could he serve me in any way? "Had we started yet?" I asked. "Yes, we had started— above an hour now—but she was not making much way. Would I get up—this was Christmas Day." So it was; I had forgotten that. What a place to hold that inspiring festival in! Mr. Bode, who was inclined to be communicative, then added that it was blowing great guns; whereof I had abundant confirmation from my own physical sufferings, then just commencing. No, I would not—could not get up; and so, for the rest of that day, dragged on a miserable existence, many times wishing that the waters would rise and cover me. Late in the evening I fell into a kind of uneasy doze, which was balm of Gilead to the tempest-tossed landsman.

When I awoke again, it was night once more; at least, there was the dull oil-lamp swinging lazily as before. There was the same painful music, the same eternal creaking and straining, as of ship's timbers in agony. What o'clock was it? Where were we now? Better make an effort, and go up, and see how we were getting on—it was so lonely down here. Come in!

Here the door was opened, and Mr. Bode, the mate, presented himself. It was a bad night, Mr. Bode said— a very bad night. He had come to tell me we were off the Head at last. He thought I might care to know.

"I am glad to hear it," I said faintly, "it will be something smoother in the open sea."

He shook his head. "No open sea for us to-night; no, nor to-morrow night most likely."

"What is all this mystery?" said I, now recollecting the captain's strange allusions at the inn door. "What do you mean?"

"It is Jan Fagel's night," said he, solemnly. "He comes into the bay to-night. An hour more of the wind, and we should have been clear. But we did what we could— a man can do no more than his best."

"But who is Jan Fagel?"

"You never heard?"

"Never. Tell me about him."

"Well," said he, "I shan't be wanted on deck for some time yet, so I may as well be here." And Mr. Bode settled himself in one of the canons' stalls, thus retiring into the shadow, and began the history of Jan Fagel and his vessel.

"You have never heard of the famous brig *Maelstrom*, once on a time well known in these roads? No, for you have not been much about here, I dare say; and it is only old sea-folk like myself that would care to talk to you of such things. But I can tell you this: There's not a sailor along the coast that hasn't the story, though it's now—let me see—a good hundred years since she made her last cruise. Why, I recollect when I was a boy, the old hull lying on the sands and breaking up with every tide—for she came to that end after all, the famous *Maelstrom*, Captain Jan Fagel, commander. I have been told there never was such a boat for foul weather, but that was when he was on board of her. He was a terrible man, was Captain Fagel, and would turn wild when a gale got up; and as the wind blew harder, so he grew wilder, until at last it seemed as if he had gone mad altogether. Why, there was one night my father used to tell of, when there was a great thunderstorm, and the sea was washing over the lighthouses—the most awful night he ever was out in; it was said that when the flashes came, Captain Jan had been seen dancing and skipping upon his deck. Many of his sailors told afterwards how they heard his mad shrieks above the roaring of the wind! Some said he had sold himself to the Evil One, which I think myself more than likely, for he cared neither for God nor man.

"Well, sir, Captain Fagel took first to the smuggling trade; and soon he and his famous brig became known all along the coast, from Hoek up to Helder—ay, and beyond that. But he was seen oftenest at the Head— as if he had a sort of liking for the place—and always came and went in a storm. So that when the Zuyder was like a boiling cauldron, and the water running over the lighthouse galleries, old sailors would look up in the wind's eye and say, 'Captain Fagel's running a cargo to-night.' At last it came to this, that whenever he was seen off Helder, he was thought to bring a storm with him. And then they would shake their heads, and say Captain Fagel was abroad that night. Soon he grew tired of this work—it was too quiet for him—so he turned Rover and ran up the black flag. He still kept his old fashion of bearing down in a gale; and many a poor disabled craft that was struggling hard to keep herself afloat, would see the black hull of the *Maelstrom* coming down upon her in the storm, and so would perish miserably upon the rocks. He was no true sailor, sir, that captain, but a low pirate; and he came to a pirate's end. And this was the way he fell upon his last cruise, just off Helder Head yonder.

"There was a certain councillor of the town who had many times crossed him in his schemes, and had once been near taking him. Fagel hated him like poison, and swore he would have his revenge of him, one day. But the councillor did not fear him, not a bit of him, but even offered a reward to whoever would take or destroy Captain Fagel and his vessel. When the captain came to hear of this he fell to raving and foaming at the mouth, and then swore a great oath upon his own soul that he would be revenged of the councillor. And this was the way he went about it:

"The councillor had a fair, young wife, Madame Elde, whom he had brought out of France some years before, and whom he loved exceedingly—foolishly, some said —for a man of his years. They and their little girl lived together at a place called Loo, and no family could be happier. Jan Fagel knew the place well, and laid his devilish plans accordingly. So, as usual, on one of his wild, stormy nights, the brig was seen standing in to shore—for no good purpose, as everybody guessed. How he and his mad crew got to land was never accounted for—but this is certain, they broke into the house at Loo and dragged Madame Elde and her child from their beds, and forced them down to their boats. The councillor was away in the city; but Captain Jan knew well enough how he loved his wife, and chose this way of torturing him. An old fisherman, who lived hard by the shore, said that he woke up suddenly in the night, and heard their screams; but they were too many for him, or he would have gone out. He was an old man, and it was only natural. They then pulled away for the ship, he standing up and screaming at the waves like a fiend incarnate, as he was. How the poor passengers ever got alive on board was a miracle, for the waves came dashing over the bows of the boat, where they were lying, at every stroke.

"Now it fell out, that at this time there was a British frigate cruising about these parts, for Captain Fagel had a short time before this fired into an English vessel. The frigate was, therefore, keeping a sharp look-out for the brig, and had been looking into all the creeks and harbours along the coasts, when she was caught in this very storm—of Captain Fagel's raising. Just as she was struggling round the Head, she came upon the *Maelstrom*, taking on board her boat's crew.

" 'Let go all clear!' they heard him cry, even above the storm—and then they saw the dark hull swing round and set off along shore, where it was hard for the frigate to follow. As for Jan Fagel, if ever Satan entered into a man in this life, he must have possessed him that night! They could hear him from the other vessel, as he shrieked with delight, and swore, and bounded along his deck, when other men could scarcely keep their feet. Why, sir, one time he was seen on the edge of the taffrail, his eyes looking in the dark like two burning coals! No doubt he would have got away from them after all—for there was no better mariner in those seas—when just as he was coming round a point, they heard a crash, and down came his topmast upon his deck. The sailors rushed to clear away the wreck.

" 'Bring up the woman,' he roared through his trumpet. 'Bring up the woman and child, you sea imps!' Though his ship was in danger, he thought of the councillor. Some of them rushed down into the hold, and came up in a moment with Madame Elde and the little girl. She was quite scared and sank down upon the deck, as if she were insensible.

" 'A handsome creature, sir,' they said—even some of those savages felt for her. They heard her saying over and over again to herself:

" 'O, such a Christmas night! Such a Christmas night!'

"He overheard her.

" 'Ah, ah! witch! You shall have a merry Christmas. Never fear. So should your husband—curse him—if we had him here.'

"She started up with a scream when she heard him speaking. And they saw her standing, with her long black hair blown back by the wind and her arms out, as if she were praying. 'Where shall Thy judgments find this man?'

" 'Here, witch! Look for me here on a stormy night— any night; next Christmas, if you like. Hi, lads! Get a sail here, and send them over the side.'

"Even those ruffians hung back, for it was too awful a night for them to add murder to their other sins. So, with many oaths, Captain Fagel went forward himself to seize the lady.

" 'He shall meet me before the judgment seat,' said she, still praying.

" 'Cant away, sorceress! Come back here of a stormy

107

night, and I'll meet you; I'm not afraid,' and he laughed long and loud.

"Then he flung the wet sail round them, and with his own hands cast them into the sea. The storm came on fiercer than ever, and they thought that the ship's timbers were going to part. But Jan Fagel strode about his deck and gave his orders, and she bore up well before the wind. It seemed that no harm could come to that ship when he was on board of her. As for the frigate, she had long since got away into the open sea. But the lady's words were not to be in vain, for just as he was doing one of his mad bounds along the poop, his foot caught in a coil of rope, and he went over with an unearthly scream into the black, swollen sea. All the crew ran to look out after him, but, strange to tell, without so much as thinking of casting him a rope. It seemed as if they had lost their sense for a time, and could only stand there looking into the waves that had swept him off. Just then the wind went down a little, and they heard a voice high in the mainmast-top as if someone were calling, and these words came to them very clear and distinct: 'Yo, yo! Jan Fagel, yo!' Then all the crew at the vessel's side, as if they had caught some of his own devilish spirit, could not keep themselves from giving out, in a great wild chorus, 'Yo, yo! Jan Fagel, yo!' Once more the voice came from the mainmast-top, calling, 'Yo, yo! Jan Fagel, yo!' and again the crew answered, louder than before, as if they were possessed. He was seen no more after that.

"The memory of that night never left that wicked

crew; and many of them, when dying quietly in their beds long after, started up with that cry, as though they were answering a call, and so passed away to their last account.

"Every year, as sure as Christmas night comes round, Jan Fagel comes into the bay to keep his word with Madame Elde. And any ship that is off the Head then must wait and beat about until midnight, when he goes away.

"But they are wanting me on deck," said Mr. Bode, looking at his watch. "I have stayed too long as it is."

Mr. Bode hastily departed, leaving me to ponder over his wild legend. Ruminating upon it and listening to the rushing of the water close to my ear, I fell off again in a sleep and began to dream; and, of course, dreamed of Captain Jan Fagel.

It was a wild and troubled sleep that I had, and I am sure, if anyone had been standing near, they would have seen me starting and turning uneasily, as if in grievous trouble. First, I thought I was ashore again, in a sheltered haven, safely delivered from all this wretched tossing. And I recollect how inexpressibly delightful the feeling of repose was, after all these weary labours. By-and-by, I remarked low-roofed old-fashioned houses all about, seemingly of wood, with little galleries running round the windows. And I saw stately burghers walking in dresses centuries old, and ladies with great round frills about their necks, and looking very stiff and majestic, sat and talked to the burghers. They were coming in and out of the queer houses, and some passed quite close to me, saluting me, as they did so, very graciously. One thing seemed very strange to me. They had all a curious dried look about their faces, and a sort of stony cast in their eyes, which I could not make out. Still they came and went, and I looked on and wondered. Suddenly I saw the little Dutch houses and the figures all quivering and getting indistinct, and gradually the picture faded away until it grew slowly into the shape of the cabin where I was now lying. There it was, all before me, with the canons' stalls and the dull swinging lamp, and I myself leaning on one hand in the carved crib, and thinking what a weary voyage this was! How monotonous the rushing sound of the water! Then my dream went on, and it seemed to me that I took note of a canon's stall in the centre, something larger and better-fashioned than the others—the dean's, most likely, I concluded wisely, when he comes to service. And then on that hint, as it were, I seemed to travel away over the waters to ancient aisles, and tracery and soft ravishing music, and snowy figures seen afar off amid duskily clouds of incense. In time, too, all that faded away, and I was back again in the oak cabin, with the sickly yellow light suffusing everything and a dark misty figure sitting right opposite. He caused me no surprise or astonishment, and I received him there as a matter of course, as people do in dreams. I had seen figures like him somewhere. In Rembrandt's pictures, was it? Most likely; for there was the large broad hat, and the stiff white collar and tassels and the dark jerkin, only there was a rusty, mouldering look about his garments that seemed very strange to me. He had an ancient sword, too, on which he leaned his arm; and so sat there motionless, looking on the ground. He sat that way I don't know how long: I, as it seemed to me, studying him intently: when suddenly the rushing sound ceased, and there came a faint cry across the waters, as from afar off. It was the old cry: "Yo, yo! Jan Fagel, yo!" Then I saw the figure raise its head suddenly, and the yellow light fell upon his face— such a mournful, despairing face!—with the same stony gaze I had seen in the others. Again the fearful cry came—nearer, as it seemed; and I saw the figure rise up slowly and walk across the cabin to the door. As he passed me he turned his dead, lac-lustre eyes full upon me, and looked at me for an instant. Never shall I forget that moment. It was as if a horrid weight was pressing on me. I felt such agony that I awoke with a start, and found myself sitting up and trembling all over. But at that instant, whether the dreamy influence had not wholly passed away, or whatever was the reason I don't know, I can swear that, above the rushing sound of the waves and the whistling of the wind, I heard that ghostly chorus, "Yo, yo! Jan Fagel, yo!" quite clear and distinct.

CHAPTER IV

An old seaman in the Surf-boat sang this ballad, as his
story, to a curious sort of tuneful no-tune, which
none of the rest could remember afterwards:

I have seen a fiercer tempest,
   Known a louder whirlwind blow.
I was wreck'd off red Algiers
   Six-and-thirty years ago.
Young I was—and yet old seamen
   Were not strong or calm as I;
While life held such treasures for me,
   I felt sure I could not die.

Life I struggled for—and saved it;
  Life alone—and nothing more;
Bruised, half dead, alone and helpless,
  I was cast upon the shore.
I fear'd the pitiless rocks of Ocean;
  So the great sea rose—and then
Cast me from her friendly bosom,
  On the pitiless hearts of men.

Gaunt and dreary ran the mountains
  With black gorges up the land;
Up to where the lonely Desert
  Spreads her burning dreary sand:
In the gorges of the mountains,
  On the plain beside the sea,
Dwelt my stern and cruel masters,
  The black Moors of Barbary.

Ten long years I toil'd among them,
  Hopeless—as I used to say;
Now I know Hope burnt within me
  Fiercer, stronger, day by day:
Those dim years of toil and sorrow,
  Like one long dark dream appear;
One long day of weary waiting;
  Then each day was like a year.

How I curst the land—my prison;
  How I curst the serpent sea,
And the Demon Fate, that shower'd
  All her curses upon me:
I was mad, I think—God pardon
  Words so terrible and wild—
This voyage would have been my last one,
  For I left a wife and child.

Never did one tender vision
  Fade away before my sight,
Never once through all my slavery,
  Burning day or dreary night;
In my soul it lived, and kept me,
  Now I feel, from black despair,
And my heart was not quite broken,
  While they lived and blest me there.

When at night my task was over,
  I would hasten to the shore;
(All was strange and foreign inland,
  Nothing I had known before).
Strange look'd the bleak mountain passes,
  Strange the red glare and black shade,
And the Oleanders, waving
  To the sound the fountains made.

Then I gazed at the great Ocean,
  Till she grew a friend again;
And because she knew old England,
  I forgave her all my pain:
So the blue still sky above me,
  With its white clouds fleecy fold,
And the glimmering stars (though brighter),
  Look'd like home and days of old.

And a calm would fall upon me;
  Worn perhaps with work and pain,
The wild hungry longing left me,
  And I was myself again:
Looking at the silver waters,
  Looking up at the far sky,
Dreams of home and all I left there
  Floated sorrowfully by.

A fair face, but pale with sorrow,
　　With blue eyes, brimful of tears,
And the little red mouth, quivering
　　With a smile, to hide its fears;
Holding out her baby towards me,
　　From the sky she look'd on me;
So it was that I last saw her,
　　As the ship put out to sea.

Sometimes (and a pang would seize me
　　That the years were floating on)
I would strive to paint her, alter'd,
　　And the little baby gone;
She no longer young and girlish,
　　The child, standing by her knee,
And her face, more pale and sadden'd
　　With the weariness for me.

Then I saw, as night grew darker,
　　How she taught my child to pray,
Holding its small hands together,
　　For its father, far away;
And I felt her sorrow, weighing
　　Heavier on me than mine own;
Pitying her blighted spring-time,
　　And her joy so early flown.

Till upon my hands (now harden'd
　　With the rough harsh toil of years),
Bitter drops of anguish, falling,
　　Woke me from my dream, to tears;
Woke me as a slave, an outcast,
　　Leagues from home, across the deep;
So—though you may call it childish—
　　So I sobb'd myself to sleep.

Well, the years sped on—my sorrow
  Calmer, and yet stronger grown,
Was my shield against all suffering,
  Poorer, meaner, than her own.
So my cruel master's harshness
  Fell upon me all in vain,
Yet the tale of what we suffer'd
  Echo'd back from main to main.

You have heard in a far country
  Of a self-devoted band,
Vow'd to rescue Christian captives
  Pining in a foreign land.
And these gentle-hearted strangers
  Year by year go forth from Rome,
In their hands the hard-earn'd ransom
  To restore some exiles home.

I was freed: they broke the tidings
  Gently to me; but indeed
Hour by hour sped on, I knew not
  What the words meant—I was freed
Better so, perhaps, while sorrow
  (More akin to earthly things)
Only strains the sad heart's fibres—
  Joy, bright stranger, breaks the strings.

Yet at last it rush's upon me,
  And my heart beat full and fast;
What were now my years of waiting,
  What was all the dreary past?
Nothing, to the impatient throbbing
  I must bear across the sea:
Nothing to the eternal hours
  Still between my home and me.

How the voyage pass'd, I know not;
    Strange it was once more to stand,
With my countrymen around me,
    And to clasp an English hand.
But, through all, my heart was dreaming
    Of the first words I should hear,
In the gentle voice that echo'd,
    Fresh as ever, on my ear.

Should I see her start of wonder,
    And the sudden truth arise,
Flushing all her face and lightening
    The dimm'd splendour of her eyes?
O! to watch the fear and doubting
    Stir the silent depths of pain,
And the rush of joy—then melting
    Into perfect peace again.

And the child!—but why remember
    Foolish fancies that I thought?
Every tree and every hedgerow
    From the well-known past I brought:
I would picture my dear cottage,
    See the crackling wood-fire burn,
And the two beside it, seated
    Watching, waiting, my return.

So, at last we reach'd the harbour.
    I remember nothing more
Till I stood, my sick heart throbbing
    With my hand upon the door.
There I paused—I heard her speaking;
    Low, soft, murmuring words she said;
Then I first knew the dumb terror
    I had had, lest she were dead.

It was evening in late autumn,
  And the gusty wind blew chill;
Autumn leaves were falling round me,
  And the red sun lit the hill.
Six-and-twenty years are vanish'd
  Since then—I am old and grey—
But I never told to mortal
  What I saw, until this day.

She was seated by the fire,
  In her arms she held a child,
Whispering baby-words caressing,
  And then, looking up, she smiled.
Smiled on him who stood beside her—
  O! the bitter truth was told!
In her look of trusting fondness,
  I had seen the look of old.

But she rose and turn'd towards me
  (Cold and dumb I waited there),
With a shriek of fear and terror,
  And a white face of despair.
He had been an ancient comrade—
  Not a single word we said,
While we gazed upon each other,
  He the living—I the dead!

I drew nearer, nearer to her,
  And I took her trembling hand,
Looking on her white face, looking
  That her heart might understand,
All the love and all the pity
  That my lips refused to say!
I thank God no thought save sorrow
  Rose in our crush'd hearts that day.

Bitter tears that desolate moment,
   Bitter, bitter tears we wept,
We three broken hearts together,
   While the baby smiled and slept.
Tears alone—no words were spoken,
   Till he—till her husband said
That my boy (I had forgotten
   The poor child), that he was dead.

Then at last I rose, and, turning,
   Wrung his hand, but made no sign;
And I stopp'd and kiss'd her forehead
   Once more, as if she were mine.
Nothing of farewell I utter'd,
   Save in broken words to pray
That God in His great love would bless her—
   Then in silence pass'd away.

Over the great restless ocean
   For twenty-and-six years I roam;
All my comrades, old and weary,
   Have gone back to die at home.
Home! yes, I shall reach a haven,
   I, too, shall reach home and rest;
I shall find her waiting for me
   With our baby on her breast.

CHAPTER V

WHILE the foregoing story was being told, I had kept my eye fixed upon little Willy Lindsey, a young Scotch boy (one of the two apprentices), who had been recommended to Captain Ravender's care by a friend in Glasgow, and very sad it was to see the expression of his face. All the early part of the voyage he had been a favourite in the ship. The ballads he sang, and the curious old stories he told, made him a popular visitor in the cabin, no less than among the people. Though only entered as apprentice seaman, Captain Ravender had kept him as much about him as he could; and I am bold to say, the lad's affection for Captain Ravender was as sincere as if he had been one of his own blood. Even before the wreck, a change had taken place in his manner. He grew silent and thoughtful. Mrs. Atherfield and Miss Coleshaw, who had been very kind to him, observed the alteration, and bantered him on the melancholy nature of the songs he sang to them, and the sad air with which he went about the duties of the vessel. I asked him if anything had occurred to make him dull, but he put me off with a laugh, and at last told me that he was thinking about his home; for, said he, a certain anniversary was coming soon, "and maybe I'll tell you," he added, "why the expectation of it makes me so sorrowful."

He was a nice, delicate, almost feminine-looking boy, of sixteen or seventeen; the son of a small farmer in Ayrshire, as Captain Ravender's Glasgow friend had told him and, as usual with his countrymen, a capital hand at letters and accounts. He had brought with him a few books, chiefly of the wild and supernatural kind, and it seemed as if he had given way to his imagination more than was quite healthy, perhaps, for the other faculties of his mind. But we all set down his delight and belief in ghost stories and such like, to the superstition of his country, where the folks seem to make up for being the most matter-of-fact people in Europe in the affairs of this world, by being the wildest and most visionary inquirers into the affairs of the next. Willy had been useful to all departments on board. The steward had employed him at his ledger, Captain Ravender at his reckonings and, as to the passengers, they had made quite a friend and companion of the youth.

So I watched his looks, as I've said before, and I now beckoned Willy to come to my side, that I might keep him as warm as I could. At first he either did not perceive my signal, or was too apathetic or too deep sunk in his own thoughts to act upon it. But the carpenter, who sat next him, seeing my motion, helped him across the boat, and I put my arm round his shoulders.

"Bear up, Willy," I said, "you're young and strong, and, with the help of Heaven, we shall all live to see our friends again."

The boy's eye brightened with hope for a moment, then he shook his head and said:

"You're very kind to say so, sir; but it canna be—at least for me."

The night was now closing fast in, but there was still light enough to see his face. It was quite calm, and wore a sort of smile. Everybody listened to hear what the poor laddie said, and I whispered to him:

"You promised to tell me why you were depressed by the coming of an anniversary, Willy. When is it?"

"It's to-night," he said, with a solemn voice. "And O! how different this is from what it used to be! It's the birthday o' my sister Jean."

"Come, tell us all about it," I said. "Maybe, speaking it out openly will ease your mind. Here, rest on my shoulder. Now say on."

We all tried to catch his words, and he began:

"It's two years ago, this very day, since we had such a merry night of it in my father's house at home. He was a farmer in a sma' way up among the hills above the Doon, and had the lands on a good tack, and was thought a richer man than any of his neighbours. There was only Jean and me o' the family; and I'm thinking nobody was ever so happy or well cared for as I was a' the time I was young. For my mither would let me want for nothing, and took me on her knee and tauld me long histories o' the Bruce and Wallace; and strange adventures with the warlocks; and sang me a' Burns' songs, forbye reading me the grand auld stories out o' the Bible about the death o' Goliath and the meeting o' King Saul and the Witch of Endor. Jean was a kind o' mither to me, too; for she was five years older, and spoilt me as much as she could. She was so bonny, it was a pleasure to look at her, and she helpit in the dairy, and often milkt the cows hersel'; and in the winter nights sat by the side o' the bleezy fire and turned the reel or span, keepin' time wi' some lang ballad about cruel Ranken coming in and killing Lady Margaret, or the ship that sailed away to Norway wi' Sir Patrick Spence, and sank wi' all the crew. The schoolmaster came up, when he was able, to gi'e me lessons; and as the road was long, and the nights were sometimes dark, it soon grew into the common custom for him to come up ow're the hills on Friday, when the school was skailt, and stay till the Monday morning. He was a young man that had been intended for a minister, but the college expenses had been too much, and he had settled down as the parish teacher at Shalloch; and we always called him Dominie Blair. All the week through, we looked for the Dominie's coming. Jean and I used to go and meet him at the bend o' the hill, where he came off from the high road, and he began his lessons to me in botany the moment we turned towards home. I noticed that he aye required the specimens that grew at the side o' the burns that ran down valleys a good way off; but I was very vain in my running, and used to rush down the gully and gather the flower or weed, and overtake the two before they had walked on a mile. So you see, sir, it was na long before it was known all over the countryside that Dominie Blair was going to marry my sister Jean. Everybody thought it a capital match, for Jean had beauty and siller, and Mr. Blair was the cleverest man in the county, and had the promise of the mastership of a school in the East country, with ninety pounds a year. Our house grew happier now than ever; and when Jean's birthday came round, there was a gathering from far and near to do honour to the bonniest and kindest lass in all the parish. The minister himsel' came up on his pony, and drank prosperity to the young folks at the door; and inside at night there was a supper for all the neighbours, and John Chalmers played on the fiddle, and a' the rest of us sang songs, and danced and skirled like mad; and at last when Jean's health was drank, with many wishes for her happiness, up she gets and lays her arms round my auld mither's neck, and bursts out into a great passion o' tears; and when she recovered herself, she said she would never be so happy anywhere else, and that weel or ill, dead or alive—in the body or in the spirit—she would aye come back on that night and look in on the hame where she had spent sae sunshiny a life. Some o' them laughed at the wild

124

affection she showed, and some took it seriously, and thought she had tied herself down by ow'r solemn a bargain; but in a wee while the mirth and frolicking gaed on as before, and all the company confessed it was the happiest evening they had ever spent in their lives. Do you ken Loch Luart, sir?—a wee bit water that stretches across between the Lureloch and the Breelen? Ah! the grand shadows that pass along it when you stand on the north side and look over to the hill. There's a great blackness settled upon the face, as if the sun had died away from the heavens altogether, till when he comes round the corner o' the mountain, a glorious procession o' sunbeams and colours taks its course across the whole length o' the water, and all the hill-sides give out a kind o' glow, and at last the loch seems all on fire and you can scarcely look at it for the brightness. A small skiff was kept at the side, for it saved the shepherds miles o' steep climbing to get from flock to flock, as it cut off two or three miles o' the distance between our house and Shalloch. One Friday, soon after the merry meeting at Jean's birthday, she set off as usual to meet Mr. Blair. How far she went, nothing was ever seen or heard o' them from that day to this; only the skiff on Loch Luart was found keel up, and the prints o' feet that answered to their size were seen on the wet bank. Nothing wad persuade my mother for many a day that she wasna coming back. When she heard a step at the door, she used to flush up with a great redness in her cheek, and run to let her in. Then when she saw it was a stranger, she left the door open and came back into the kitchen without sayin' a word. My father spoke very little, but sometimes he seemed to forget that Jean was taken away, and called for her to come to him in a cheery voice, as he used to do; and then, wi' a sudden shake o' his head, he remembered that she was gone, and passed away to his work as if his heart was broken. And other things came on to disturb him now, for some bank, or railway, or something o' the kind, where he had bought some shares, failed with a great crash, and he was called on to make up the loss; and he grew careless about everything that happened, and the horses and carts were seized for debt, and a' the cows except two were taken away, and the place began to go to wrack and ruin; and at last Jean's birthday cam' round again. But we never spoke about it the whole day long, though none of the three thought of anything else. My father pretended to be busy in the field; my mother span—never letting the thread out o' her hand; and as for me, I wandered about the hills from early morning, and only came back when the dark night began. All through the lengthening hours we sat and never spoke; but sometimes my father put a fresh supply of peats upon the fire and stirred it up into a blaze, as if it pleased him to see the great sparkles flying up the chimney. At last my mother, all of a sudden, ceased her spinning, and said: 'Hark! do you no' hear somebody outside?' And we listened without getting up from our seats. We heard a sound as if somebody was slipping by on tip-toe on the way to the Byre, and then we heard a low, wailing sound, as if the person was trying to restrain some great sorrow; and immediately we heard the same footstep, as if it were lost in snow, coming up to the house. My mither stood up wi' her hand stretched out, and looked at the window. Outside the pane—where the rose tree has grown sae thick it half hides the lower half—we heard a rustling, as if somebody was putting aside the leaves, and then, when a sudden flicker o' the flame threw its light upon the casement, we saw the faint image o' a bonny pale face—very sad to look on—wi' lang tresses o' yellow hair hanging straight down the cheeks, as if it was dripping wet, and heard low, plaintive sobs; but nothing that we could understand. My mither ran forward, as if to embrace the visitor, and cried, 'Jean! Jean! O, let me speak to you, my bairn!' But the flame suddenly died away in the grate, and we saw nothing mair. But we all knew now that Jean had been drowned in Loch Luart, and that she minded the promise she had made to come and see the auld house upon her birthday."

Here the boy paused in his narrative for a moment, and I felt his breath coming and going very quick, as if his strength was getting rapidly exhausted.

"Rest a while, Willy," I said, "and try, if you can, to sleep."

But nothing could restrain him from finishing his tale.

"Na, na! I canna rest upon your arm, sir. I ha'e wark to do, and it maun be done this night—wae's me! I didna think, last year at this time, that ever I wad be here." He looked round with a shudder at the coiling waves that rose high at the side of the boat and shut out the faint glimmer that still lingered on the horizon line. "So Jean was drowned, ye see," he continued, "and couldna put foot inside—for a' they can do is to look in and see what's doing at the auld fireside through the window. But even this was a comfort to my mither; and as I saw how glad it made her to have this assurance that she wasna forgotten, I made her the same promise that Jean had done on her birthday: ill or weel, happy or miserable, in the body or in the spirit, I wad find my way to the farm-house, and gi'e her some sign that I loved her as I had always done. And now I ken what they're doing as if I was at hame. They're sitting sad and lonely in the silent kitchen. My father puts fresh peats upon the grate, and watches their flame as it leaps and crackles up the fireplace; and my mither—Ah!"— here he stretched forward as if to see some object before him more distinctly—"ah! she's spinning, spinning as if to keep herself from thinking, and tears are running down her face; and I see the cheery fire, and the heather bed in the corner, and the round table in the middle, and the picture o' Abraham and Isaac on the wall, and my fishing-rod hung up aboon the mantelpiece, and my herding-staff, and my old blue bonnet. But how cold it is, sir," he went on, turning to me. "I felt a touch on my shoulder just now that made me creep as if the hand were ice; and I looked up and saw the same face we had noticed last year; and I feel the clammy fingers yet, and they go downward—downward, chilling me a' the way till my blood seems frozen, and I canna speak. O, for anither look at the fire and the warm cosy room, and my father's white head, and my puir auld mither's een!"

So saying, he tried to rise, and seemed to be busy putting aside something that interfered with his view.

"The rose tree!" he said. "It's thicker than ever, and I canna see clear!" At last he appeared to get near the object he sought; and, after altering his position, as if to gain a perfect sight, he said: "I see them a' again. O, mither! Turn your face this way, for ye see I've kept my word; and we're both here. Jean's beside me, and very cold—and we darena come in." He watched for about a minute, still gazing intently, and then, with a joyous scream, he exclaimed: "She sees me—she sees me! Did na ye hear her cry? O mither, mither! tak' me to your arms, for I'm chilled wi' the salt water, and naething will make me warm again."

I tightened my hold of poor Willy as he spoke, for he gradually lost his power, and at last lay speechless with his head on my shoulder. I concealed from the rest the sad event that occurred in a few minutes, and kept the body hidden till the darkest part of the night, closely wrapped in my cloak.

PART THREE
"The Deliverance"

CHAPTER I

WHEN the sun rose on the twenty-seventh day of our calamity, the first question that I secretly asked myself was: "How many more mornings will the stoutest of us live to see?" I had kept count, ever since we took to the boats, of the days of the week, and I knew that we had now arrived at another Thursday. Judging by my own sensations (and I believe I had as much strength left as the best man among us), I came to the conclusion that, unless the mercy of Providence interposed to effect our deliverance, not one of our company could hope to see another morning after the morning of Sunday.

Two discoveries that I made—after redeeming my promise overnight, to serve out with the morning whatever eatable thing I could find—helped to confirm me in my gloomy view of our future prospects. In the first place, when the few coffee berries left, together with a small allowance of water, had been shared all round, I found on examining the lockers that not one grain of provision remained, fore or aft, in any part of the boat, and that our stock of fresh water was reduced to not much more than would fill a wine-bottle. In the second place, after the berries had been shared, and the water equally divided, I noticed that the sustenance thus administered produced no effect whatever, even of the most momentary kind, in raising the spirits of the passengers (excepting in one case) or in rallying the strength of the crew. The exception was Mr. Rarx. This tough and greedy old sinner seemed to wake up from the trance he had lain in so long, when the smell of the berries and water was under his nose. He swallowed his share with a gulp that a younger and better man in the boat might have envied, and went maundering on to himself afterwards, as if he had got a new lease of life. He fancied now that he was digging a gold-mine, all by himself, and going down bodily straight through the earth at the rate of thirty or forty miles an hour. "Leave me alone," says he, "leave me alone. The lower I go, the richer I get. Down I go! Down, down, down, down, till I burst out at the other end of the world in a shower of gold!" So he went on, kicking feebly with his heels from time to time against the bottom of the boat.

But, as for all the rest, it was a pitiful and dreadful sight to see of how little use their last shadow of a meal was to them. I myself attended, before anybody else was served, to the two poor women. Miss Coleshaw shook her head faintly, and pointed to her throat, when I offered her the few berries that fell to her share. I made a shift to crush them up fine and mix them with a little water, and got her to swallow that miserable drop of drink with the greatest difficulty. When it was down there came no change for the better over her face. Nor did she recover, for so much as a moment, the capacity to speak, even in a whisper. I next tried Mrs. Atherfield. It was hard to wake her out of the half-swooning, half-sleeping condition in which she lay, and harder still to get her to open her lips when I put the tin-cup to them. When I had at last prevailed on her to swallow her allowance, she shut her eyes again and fell back into her old position. I saw her lips moving, and, putting my ear close to them, caught some of the words she was murmuring to herself. She was still dreaming of the Golden Lucy. She and the child were walking somewhere by the banks of a lake, at the time when the buttercups are out. The Golden Lucy was gathering the buttercups and making herself a watch-chain out of them, in imitation of the chain that her mother wore. They were carrying a little basket with them, and were going to dine together in a great hollow tree growing on the banks of the lake. To get this pretty picture painted on one's mind as I got it, while listening to the poor mother's broken words, and then to look up at the haggard faces of the men in the boat, and at the wild ocean rolling all round us, was such a change from fancy to reality as it has fallen, I hope, to few men's lot to experience.

My next thought, when I had done my best for the women, was for the captain. I was free to risk losing my own share of water, if I pleased, so I tried, before tasting it myself, to get a little between his lips; but his teeth were fast clenched, and I had neither strength nor skill to open them. The faint warmth still remained, thank God, over his heart—but, in all other respects he lay beneath us like a dead man. In covering him up again as comfortably as I could, I found a bit of paper crunched in one of his hands, and took it out. There was some writing on it, but not a word was readable. I supposed, poor fellow, that he had been trying to write some last instructions for me, just before he dropped at his post. If they had been ever so easy to read, they would have been of no use now. To follow instructions we must have had some power to shape the boat's course in a given direction—and this, which he had been gradually losing for some days past, we had now lost altogether.

I had hoped that the serving out of the refreshment would have put a little modicum of strength into the arms of the men at the oars; but, as I have hinted, this hope turned out to be perfectly fruitless. Our last mockery of a meal, which had done nothing for the passengers, did nothing either for the crew—except to aggravate the pangs of hunger in the men who were still strong enough to feel them. While the weather held moderate, it was not of much consequence if one or two of the rowers kept dropping, in turn, into a kind of faint sleep over their oars. But if it came on to blow again (and we could expect nothing else in those seas and at that time of the year), how was I to steer, when the blades of the oars were out of the water ten times as often as they were in? The lives which we had undergone such suffering to preserve would have been lost in an instant by the swamping of the boat, if the wind has risen on the morning of Thursday, and had caught us trying to row any longer.

Feeling this, I resolved, while the weather held moderately fine, to hoist the best substitute for a sail that we could produce, and to drive before the wind, on the chance (the last we had to hope for) of a ship picking us up. We had only continued to use the oars up to this time, in order to keep the course which the captain had pointed out as likeliest to bring us near the land. Sailing had been out of the question from the first, the masts and suits of sails belonging to each boat having been out of them at the time of the wreck and having gone down with the ship. This was an accident which there was no need to deplore, for we were too crowded from the first to admit of handling the boats properly, under their regular press of sail, in anything like rough weather.

Having made up my mind on what it was necessary to do, I addressed the men, and told them that any notion of holding longer on our course with the oars was manifestly out of the question, and dangerous to all on board, as their own common sense might tell them, in the state to which the stoutest arms among us were now reduced. They looked round on each other as I said that, each man seeming to think his neighbour weaker than himself. I went on, and told them that we must take advantage of our present glimpse of moderate weather, and hoist the best sail we could set up and drive before the wind, in the hope that it might please God to direct us in the way of some ship before it was too late. "Our only chance, my men," I said in conclusion, "is the chance of being picked up; and in these desolate seas one point of the compass is just as likely a point for our necessities as another. Half of you keep the boat before the sea, the other half bring out your knives, and do as I tell you." The prospect of being relieved from the oars struck the wandering attention of the men directly, and they said, "Ay, ay, sir!" with something like a faint reflection of their former readiness, when the good ship was under their feet and the messcans were filled with plenty of wholesome food.

Thanks to Captain Ravender's forethought in providing both boats with a coil of rope, we had our lashings, and the means of making what rigging was wanted, ready to hand. One of the oars was made fast to the thwart, and well stayed fore and aft, for a mast. A large pilot coat that I wore was spread, enough of sail for us. The only difficulty that puzzled me was occasioned by the necessity of making a yard. The men tried to tear up one of the thwarts, but were not strong enough. My own knife had been broken in the attempt to split a bit of plank for them, and I was almost at my wit's end, when I luckily thought of searching the captain's pockets for his knife. I found it—a fine large knife of Sheffield manufacture, with plenty of blades, and a small saw among them. With this we made a shift to saw off about a third of another oar; and then the difficulty was conquered, and we got my pilot coat hoisted on our jury-mast, and rigged it as nigh as we could to the fashion of a lug-sail.

I had looked anxiously towards the Surf-boat, while we were rigging our mast, and observed, with a feeling of great relief, that the men in her—as soon as they discovered what we were about—were wise enough to follow our example. They got on faster than we did, being less put to it for room to turn round in. We set our sails as nearly as possible about the same time, and it was well for both boats that we finished our work when we did. At noon the wind began to rise again to a stiff breeze, which soon knocked up a heavy, tumbling sea. We drove before it in a direction north and by east, keeping wonderfully dry, considering all things. The mast stood well; and the sail, small as it was, did good service in steadying the boat and lifting her easily over the seas. I felt the cold after the loss of my coat, but not so badly as I had feared, for the two men who were with me in the stern sheets sat as close as they could on either side of me, and helped with the warmth of their own bodies to keep the warmth in mine. Forward, I told off half-a-dozen of the most trustworthy of the men who could still muster strength enough to keep their eyes open, to set a watch, turn and turn about, on our frail rigging. The wind was steadily increasing, and if any accident happened to our mast, the chances were that the boat would broach-to, and that every one of us would go to the bottom.

So we drove on, all through that day, sometimes catching sight of the Surf-boat a little ahead of us, sometimes losing her altogether in the scud. How little and frail, how very different to the kind of boat that I had expected to see, she looked to my eyes now that I was out of her, and saw what she showed like on the waters for the first time! But to return to the Long-boat. The watch on the rigging was relieved every two hours, and at the same regular periods all the brightest eyes left amongst us looked out for the smallest vestige of a sail in view, and looked in vain. Among the passengers, nothing happened in the way of a change—except that Miss Coleshaw seemed to grow fainter, and that Mrs. Atherfield got restless, as if she were waking out of her long dream about the Golden Lucy.

CHAPTER II

IT got on towards sunset. The wind was rising to half
a gale. The clouds which had been heavy all over the
firmament since noon, were lifting to the westward
and leaving there, over the horizon line of the ocean,
a long strip of clear, pale greenish sky, overhung by
a cloud-bank, whose ragged edges were tipped with
burning crimson by the sun. I did not like the look of
the night, and, keeping where I was, in the forward
part of the boat, I helped the men to ease the strain off
our mast by lowering the yard a little and taking a

pull on the sheet, so as to present to the wind a smaller surface even of our small sail. Noting the wild look of the weather, and the precautions we were taking against the chance of a gale rising in the night—and being, furthermore, as I believe, staggered in their minds by the death that had taken place among them—three of the passengers struggled up in the bottom of the boat, clasped their arms round me as if they were drowning men already, and hoarsely clamoured for a last drink of water before the storm rose and sent us all to the bottom.

"Water you shall have," I said, "when I think the time has come to serve it out. The time has not come yet."

"Water, pray!" they all three groaned together. Two more passengers who were asleep, woke up, and joined the cry.

"Silence!" I said. "There are not two spoonfuls of fresh water left for each man in the boat. I shall wait three hours more for the chance of rain before I serve that out. Silence, and drop back to your places!"

They let go of me, but clamoured weakly for water still; and, this time, the voices of some of the crew joined them. At this moment, to my great alarm (for I thought they were going mad and turning violent against me), I was seized round the neck by one of the men, who had been standing up, holding on by the mast, and looking out steadily to the westward.

I raised my right hand to free myself; but before I touched him, the sight of the man's face close to mine made me drop my arm again. There was a speechless, breathless, frantic joy in it, that made all the blood in my veins stand still in a moment.

"Out with it!" I said. "Man alive, out with it, for God's sake!"

His breath beat on my cheek in hot, quick, heavy gasps, but he could not utter a word. For a moment he let go of the mast (tightening his hold on me with the other arm) and pointed out westward—then slid heavily down on to the thwart behind us.

I looked westward, and saw that one of the two trustworthy men whom I had left at the helm was on his feet looking out westward, too. As the boat rose, I fixed my eyes on the strip of clear greenish sky in the west, and on the bright line of the sea just under it. The boat dipped again before I could see anything. I squeezed my eyelids together to get the water out of them, and when we rose again looked straight into the middle of the bright sea-line. My heart bounded as if it would choke me, my tongue felt like a cinder in my mouth, my knees gave way under me. I dropped down on to the thwart, and sobbed out, with a great effort, as if I had been dumb for weeks before, and had only that instant found my speech:

"A sail! a Sail!"

The words were instantly echoed by the man in the stern sheets.

"Sail, ho!" he screeches out, turning round on us, and swinging his arms about his head like a madman.

This made three of our company who had seen the ship already, and that one fact was sufficient to remove all dread lest our eyes might have been deceiving us.

The great fear now was, not that we were deluded, but that we might come to some serious harm through the excess of joy among the people; that is to say, among such of the people as still had the sense to feel and the strength to express what they felt. I must record in my own justification, after confessing that I lost command over myself altogether on the discovery of the sail, that I was the first who set the example of self-control. I was in a manner forced to this by the crew frantically entreating me to lay-to until we could make out what course the ship was steering—a proceeding which, with the sea then running, with the heavy lading of the boat, and with such feeble substitutes for mast and sail as we possessed, must have been attended with total destruction to us all. I tried to remind the men of this, but they were in such a transport—hugging each other round the neck, and crying and laughing all in a breath— that they were not fit to listen to reason. Accordingly, I myself went to the helm again, and chose the steadiest of my two men in the after part of the boat as a guard over the sheet, with instructions to use force, if necessary, towards anyone who stretched out so much as a finger to it. The wind was rising every minute, and we had nothing for it but to scud, and be thankful to God's mercy that we had sea-room to do it in.

"It will be dark in an hour's time, sir," says the man left along with me when I took the helm again. "We have no light to show. The ship will pass us in the night. Lay to, sir! For the love of Heaven, give us all a chance, and lay to!" says he, and goes down on his knees before me, wringing his hands.

"Lay to!" says I. "Lay to, under a coat! Lay to, in a boat like this, with the wind getting up to a gale! A seaman like you talking that way! Who have I got along here with me? Sailors who know their craft, or a pack of long-shore lubbers, who ought to be turned adrift in a ferry-boat on a pond?" My heart was heavy enough, God knows, but I spoke out as loud as I could, in that light way, to try and shame the men back to their proper senses. I succeeded at least in restoring silence; and that was something in such a condition as ours.

My next anxiety was to know if the men in the Surf-boat had sighted the sail to the westward. She was still driving ahead of us, and the first time I saw her rise on the waves, I made out a signal on board—a strip of cloth fastened to a boat-hook. I ordered the man by my side to return it with his jacket tied on to the end of an oar, being anxious to see whether his agitation had calmed down and left him fit for his duty again. He followed my directions steadily, and when he had got his jacket on again, asked me to pardon him for losing his self-command in a quiet, altered voice.

I shook hands with him and gave him the helm, in proof that my confidence was restored, then stood up and turned my face to the westward once again. I looked long into the belt of clear sky, which was narrowing already as the cloud-bank above sank over it. I looked with all my heart and soul and strength. It was only when my eyes could stand the strain on them no longer that I gave in, and sat down again by the tiller. If I had not been supported by a firm trust in the mercy of

Providence, which had preserved us thus far, I am afraid I should have abandoned myself at that trying time to downright hopeless, speechless despair.

It would not express much to any but seafaring readers if I mentioned the number of leagues off that I considered the ship to be. I shall give a better idea of the terrible distance there was between us, when I say that no landsman's eye could have made her out at all, and that none of us sailors could have seen her but for the bright opening in the sky, which made even a speck on the waters visible to a mariner's experienced sight all that weary way off. When I have said this, I have said enough to render it plain to every man's understanding that it was a sheer impossibility to make out what course the ship was steering, seeing that we had no chance of keeping her in view at that closing time of day for more than another half-hour, at most. There she was, astern to leeward of us; and here were we, driving for our lives before the wind, with any means of kindling a light that we might have possessed on leaving our ship wetted through long ago, with no guns to fire as signals of distress in the darkness, and with no choice, if the wind shifted, but still to scud in any direction in which it might please to drive us. Supposing, even at the best, that the ship was steering on our course, and would overhaul us in the night, what chance had we of making our position known to her in the darkness? Truly, look at it anyhow we might from our poor mortal point of view, our prospect of deliverance seemed to be of the most utterly hopeless kind that it is possible to conceive.

The men felt this bitterly, as the cloud-bank dropped to the verge of the waters, and the sun set redly behind it. The moaning and lamenting among them was miserable to hear, when the last speck and phantom of the ship had vanished from view. Some few still swore they saw her when there was hardly a flicker of light left in the west, and only gave up looking out, and dropped down in the boat, at my express orders. I charged them all solemnly to set an example of courage to the passengers, and to trust the rest to the infinite wisdom and mercy of the Creator of us all. Some murmured, some fell to repeating scraps out of the Bible and Prayer Book, some wandered again in their minds. This went on till the darkness gathered; then a great hush of silence fell drearily over passengers and crew, and the waves and the wind hissed and howled about us, as if we were tossing in the midst of them, a boat-load of corpses already!

Twice in the forepart of the night the clouds overhead parted for a little, and let the blessed moonlight down upon us. On the first of those occasions, I myself served out the last drops of fresh water we had left. The two women—poor suffering creatures!—were past drinking. Miss Coleshaw shivered a little when I moistened her lips with the water; and Mrs. Atherfield, when I did the same for her, drew her breath with a faint, fluttering sigh, which was just enough to show that she was not dead yet. The captain still lay as he had lain ever since I got on board the boat. The others, both passengers and crew, managed for the most part to swallow their share of the water, the men being just sufficiently roused by it to get up on their knees, while the moonlight lasted, and look about wildly over the ocean for a chance of seeing the ship again. When the clouds gathered once more, they crouched back in their places with a long groan of despair. Hearing that, and dreading the effect of the pitchy darkness (to say nothing of the fierce wind and sea) on their sinking spirits, I resolved to combat their despondency, if it were still possible to contend against it, by giving them something to do. First telling them that no man could say at what time of the night the ship (in case she was steering our course) might forge ahead of us, or how near she might be when she passed, I recommended that all who had the strength should join the voices at regular intervals, and shout their loudest when the boat rose highest on the waves, on the chance of that cry of distress being borne by the wind within hearing of the watch on board the ship. It is unnecessary to say that I knew well how near it was to an absolute impossibility that this last feeble exertion on our parts could lead to any result. I only proposed it because I was driven to the end of my resources to keep up the faintest flicker of spirit among the men. They received my proposal with more warmth and readiness than I had ventured, in their hopeless state, to expect from them. Up to the turn of midnight they resolutely raised their voices with me, at intervals of from five to ten minutes, whenever the boat was tossed highest on the waves. The wind seemed to whirl our weak cries savagely out of our mouths almost before we could utter them. I, sitting astern in the boat only heard them, as it seemed, for something like an instant of time. But even that was enough to make me creep all over—the cry was so forlorn and fearful. Of all the dreadful sounds I had heard since the first striking of the ship, that shrill wail of despair—rising on the wave-tops one moment, whirled away, the next, into the black night—was the most frightful that entered my ears. There are times, even now, when it seems to be ringing in them still.

Whether our first gleam of moonshine fell upon old Mr. Rarx, while he was sleeping, and helped to upset his weak brains altogether, is more than I can say. But, for some reason or other, before the clouds parted and let the light down on us for the second time, and while we were driving along awfully through the blackest of the night, he stirred in his place, and began rambling and raving again more vehemently than ever. To hear him now—that is to say, as well as I could hear him for the wind—he was still down in his gold-mine, but laden so heavy with his precious metal that he could not get out, and was in mortal peril of being drowned by the water rising in the bottom of the shaft. So far, his maundering attracted my attention disagreeably, and did no more. But when he began—if I may say so—to take the name of the dear little dead child in vain, and to mix her up with himself and his miserly greed of gain, I got angry, and called to the men forward to give him a shake and make him hold his tongue. Whether any of them obeyed or not, I don't know—Mr. Rarx went on raving louder than ever. The shrill wind was now hardly more shrill than he. He swore he saw the white frock of our poor little lost pet fluttering in the daylight at the top of the mine, and he screamed out to her in a great fright that the gold was heavy and the water rising fast, and that she must come down quick as lightning if she meant to be in time to help him. I called again angrily to the men to silence him; and just as I did so, the clouds began to part for the second time, and the white tip of the moon grew visible.

"There she is!" screeches Mr. Rarx, and I saw him by the faint light scramble on his knees in the bottom of the boat, and wave a ragged old handkerchief up at the moon.

"Pull him down!" I called out. "Down with him, and tie his arms and legs!"

Of the men who could still move about, not one paid any attention to me. They were all upon their knees again, looking out in the strengthening moonlight for a sight of the ship.

"Quick, Golden Lucy!" screams Mr. Rarx, and creeps under the thwarts right forward into the bows of the boat. "Quick! my darling, my beauty, quick! The gold is heavy, and the water rises fast! Come down and save me, Golden Lucy! Let all the rest of the world drown, and save me! Me! me! me! me!"

He shouted these last words out at the top of his cracked, croaking voice, and got on his feet, as I conjectured (for the coat we had spread for a sail now hid him from me) in the bows of the boat. Not one of the crew so much as looked round at him, so eagerly were their eyes seeking for the ship. The man sitting by me was sunk in a deep sleep. If I had left the helm for a moment in that wind and sea, it would have been the death of every soul of us. I shouted desperately to the raving wretch to sit down. A screech that seemed to cut the very wind in two answered me. A huge wave tossed the boat's head up wildly at the same moment. I looked aside to leeward as the wash of the great roller swept by us, gleaming of a lurid, bluish-white in the moonbeams; I looked and saw, in one second of time, the face of Mr. Rarx rush past on the wave, with the foam seething in his hair and the moon shining in his eyes. Before I could draw my breath he was a hundred yards astern of us, and the night and the sea had swallowed him up and had hid his secret, which he had kept all the voyage from our mortal curiosity, for ever.

"He's gone! he's drowned!" I shouted to the men forward.

None of them took any notice; none of them left off looking out over the ocean for a sight of the ship. Nothing that I could say on the subject of our situation at that fearful time can, in my opinion, give such an idea of the extremity and the frightfulness of it, as the relation of this one fact. I leave it to speak by itself the sad and shocking truth, and pass on gladly to the telling of what happened next, at a later hour of the night.

After the clouds had shut out the moon again, the wind dropped a little and shifted a point or two, so as to shape our course nearer to the eastward. How the hours passed after that, till the dawn came, is more than I can tell. The nearer the time of daylight approached the more completely everything seemed to drop out of my mind, except the one thought of where the ship we had seen in the evening might be, when we looked for her with the morning light.

It came at last—that grey, quiet light which was to end all our uncertainty, which was to show us if we were saved, or to warn us if we were to prepare for death. With the first streak in the east, every one of the boat's company, except the sleeping and the senseless, roused up and looked out in breathless silence upon the sea. Slowly and slowly the daylight strengthened, and the darkness rolled off farther and farther before it over the face of the waters. The first pale flush of the sun flew trembling along the paths of light broken through the grey wastes of the eastern clouds. We could look clearly, we could see far; and there, ahead of us—O! merciful, bountiful providence of God!—there was the ship!

CHAPTER III

I HAVE honestly owned the truth, and confessed to human infirmity under suffering of myself, my passengers and my crew. I have earned, therefore, as I would fain hope, the right to record it to the credit of all, that the men, the moment they set eyes on the ship, poured out their whole hearts in humble thanksgiving to the Divine Mercy which had saved them from the very jaws of death. They did not wait for me to bid them do this; they did it of their own accord, in their own language, fervently, earnestly, with one will and one heart.

We had hardly made the ship out—a fine brigantine, hoisting English colours—before we observed that her crew suddenly hove her up in the wind. At first we were at a loss to understand this; but as we drew nearer, we discovered that she was getting the Surf-boat (which had kept ahead of us all through the night) alongside of her, under the lee-bow. My men tried to cheer when they saw their companions in safety, but their weak cries died away in tears and sobbing.

In another half-hour we, too, were alongside of the brigantine.

From this point, I recollect nothing very distinctly. I remember faintly many loud voices and eager faces; I remember fresh, strong willing fellows, with a colour in their cheeks and a smartness in their movements that seemed quite preternatural to me at that time, hanging over us in the rigging of the brigantine, and dropping down from her side into our boat; I remember trying with my feeble hands to help them in the difficult and perilous task of getting the two poor women and the captain on board; I remember one dark hairy giant of a man swearing that it was enough to break his heart and catching me in his arms like a child—and from that moment I remember nothing more with the slightest certainty for over a week of time.

When I came to my own senses again, in my cot on board the brigantine, my first inquiries were naturally for my fellow-sufferers. Two—a passenger in the Long-boat, and one of the crew of the Surf-boat—had sunk in spite of all the care that could be taken of them. The rest were likely, with time and attention, to recover.

Of those who have been particularly mentioned in this narrative, Mrs. Atherfield had shown signs of rallying the soonest; Miss Coleshaw, who had held out longer against exhaustion, was now the slower to recover. Captain Ravender, though slowly mending, was still not able to speak or to move in his cot without help. The sacrifices for us all which this good man had so nobly undergone, not only in the boat, but before that, when he had deprived himself of his natural rest on the dark nights that preceded the wreck of the *Golden Mary*, had sadly undermined his natural strength of constitution. He, the heartiest of all, when we sailed from England, was now, through his unwearying devotion to his duty and to us, the last to recover, the longest to linger between life and death.

My next questions (when they helped me on deck to get my first blessed breath of fresh air) related to the vessel that had saved us. She was bound to the Columbia river—a long way to the northward of the port for which we had sailed in the *Golden Mary*. Most providentially for us, shortly after we had lost sight of the brigantine in the shades of the evening, she had been caught in a squall, and had sprung her foretop-mast badly. This accident had obliged them to lay-to for some hours, while they did their best to secure the spar, and had warned them when they continued on their course to keep the ship under easy sail through the night. But for this circumstance we must, in all human probability, have been too far astern when the morning dawned to have had the slightest chance of being discovered.

Excepting always some of the stoutest of our men, the next of the Long-boat's company who was helped on deck was Mrs. Atherfield. Poor soul! When she and I first looked at each other, I could see that her heart went back to the early days of our voyage, when the Golden Lucy and I used to have our game of hide-and-seek round the mast. She squeezed my hand as hard as she could with her wasted trembling fingers, and looked up piteously in my face, as if she would like to speak to little Lucy's playfellow, but dared not trust herself; then turned away quickly and laid her head against the bulwark, and looked out upon the desolate sea that was nothing to her now but her darling's grave. I was better pleased when I saw her later in the day, sitting by Captain Ravender's cot, for she seemed to take comfort in nursing him. Miss Coleshaw soon afterwards got strong enough to relieve her at this duty; and, between them, they did the captain such a world of good, both in body and spirit, that he also got strong enough before long to come on deck and to thank me, in his old generous self-forgetful way, for having done my duty—the duty which I had learnt how to do by his example.

Hearing what our destination had been when we sailed from England, the captain of the brigantine (who had treated us with the most unremitting attention and kindness, and had been warmly seconded in his efforts for our good by all the people under his command) volunteered to go sufficiently out of his course to enable us to speak the first Californian coasting-vessel sailing in the direction of San Francisco. We were lucky in meeting with one of these sooner than we expected. Three days after parting from the kind captain of the brigantine we, the surviving passengers and crew of the *Golden Mary*, touched the firm ground once more, on the shores of California.

We were hardly collected here before we were obliged to separate again. Captain Ravender, though he was hardly yet in good travelling trim, accompanied Mrs. Atherfield inland, to see her safe under her husband's protection. Miss Coleshaw went with them, to stay with Mrs. Atherfield for a little while before she attempted to proceed with any matters of her own which had brought her to this part of the world. The rest of us, who were left behind with nothing particular to do until the captain's return, followed the passengers to the gold diggings. Some few of us had enough of the life there in a very short time. The rest seemed bitten by old Mr. Rarx's mania for gold, and insisted on stopping behind when Rames and I proposed going back to the port. We two, and five of our steadiest seamen, were all the officers and crew left to meet the captain on his return from the inland country.

He reported that he had left Mrs. Atherfield and Miss Coleshaw safe and comfortable under Mr. Atherfield's care. They sent affectionate messages to all of us, and especially (I am proud to say) to me. After hearing this good news, there seemed nothing better to do than to ship on board the first vessel bound for England. There were plenty in port, ready to sail, and only waiting for the men belonging to them who had deserted to the gold diggings. We were all snapped up eagerly and offered any rate we chose to set on our services, the moment we made known our readiness to ship for England—all, I ought to have said, except Captain Ravender, who went along with us in the capacity of passenger only.

Nothing of any moment occurred on the voyage back. The captain and I got ashore at Gravesend safe and hearty, and went up to London as fast as the train could carry us to report the calamity that had occurred to the owners of the *Golden Mary*. When that duty had been performed, Captain Ravender went back to his own house at Poplar, and I travelled to the West of England to report myself to my old father and mother.

Here I might well end all these pages of writing; but I cannot refrain from adding a few more sentences, to tell the reader what I am sure he will be glad to hear. In the summer-time of this present year eighteen hundred and fifty-six, I happened to be at New York, and having spare time on my hands and spare cash in my pocket, I walked into one of the biggest and grandest of their Ordinaries there, to have my dinner. I had hardly sat down at table, before who should I see opposite but Mrs. Atherfield, as bright-eyed and pretty as ever, with a gentleman on her right hand, and on her left—another Golden Lucy! Her hair was a shade or two darker than the hair of my poor little pet of past sad times; but in all other respects the living child reminded me so strongly of the dead, that I quite started at the first sight of her. I could not tell, if I was to try, how happy we were after dinner, or how much we had to say to each other.

I was introduced to Mrs. Atherfield's husband, and heard from him, among other things, that Miss Coleshaw was married to her old sweetheart, who had fallen into misfortunes and errors, and whom she was determined to set right by giving him the great chance in life of getting a good wife. They were settled in America, like Mr. and Mrs. Atherfield—these last and the child being on their way, when I met them, to visit a friend living in the northernmost part of the states.

With the relation of this circumstance, and with my personal testimony to the good health and spirits of Captain Ravender the last time I saw him, ends all that I have to say in connection with the subject of the Wreck of the *Golden Mary*, and the Great Deliverance of her People at Sea.

THE END